SPACE CHESS

Three days out, Jay made a major hit with the Martians. As everyone knows, those goggle-eyed, ten-tentacled, half-breathing kibitzers have stuck harder than glue to the Solar System Chess Championship for more than two centuries. Nobody outside of Mars will ever pry them loose. They are nuts about the game and many's the time I've seen a bunch of them go through all the colours of the spectrum in sheer excitement when at last somebody has moved a pawn after thirty minutes of profound cogitation . . .

MEN, MARTIANS AND MACHINES

Eric Frank Russell

A BERKLEY MEDALLION BOOK
published by
BERKLEY PUBLISHING CORPORATION

JAY SCORE

There are very good reasons for everything they do. To the uninitiated some of their little tricks and some of their regulations seem mighty peculiar—but rocketing through the cosmos isn't quite like paddling a bathtub across a farm pond, no, sir!

For instance, this stunt of using mixed crews is pretty sensible when you look into it. On the outward runs toward Mars, the Asteroids or beyond, they have white Terrestrials to tend the engines because they're the ones who perfected modern propulsion units, know most about them and can nurse them like nobody else. All ships' surgeons are black Terrestrials because for some reason none can explain no Negro gets gravity-bends or space nausea. Every outside repair gang is composed of Martians who use very little air, are tiptop metal workers and fairly immune to cosmic-ray burn.

As for the inward trips to Venus, they mix them similarly except that the emergency pilot is always a big clunker like Jay Score. There's a motive behind that; he's the one who provided it. I'm never likely to forget him. He sort of sticks in my mind, for keeps. What a character!

Destiny placed me at the top of the gangway the first time he appeared. Our ship was the *Upskadaska City*, a brand new freighter with limited passenger accommodation, registered in the Venusian space-port from which she took her name. Needless to say she was known among hardened spacemen as the *Upsydaisy*.

We were lying in the Colorado Rocket Basin, north of Denver, with a fair load aboard, mostly watch-making machinery, agricultural equipment, aeronautical jigs and tools for Upskadaska, as well as a case of radium needles for the Venusian Cancer Research Institute. There were eight passengers, all emigrating agriculturalists planning on making hay thirty million miles nearer the Sun. We had ramped the vessel and were waiting for the blow-brothers-blow siren due in forty minutes, when Jay Score arrived.

He was six feet nine, weighed at least three hundred pounds yet toted this bulk with the easy grace of a ballet dancer. A big guy like that, moving like that, was something worth watching. He came up the duralumin gangway with all the nonchalance of a tripper boarding the bus for Jackson's Creek. From his hamlike right fist dangled a rawhide case not quite big enough to contain his bed and maybe a wardrobe or two.

Reaching the top, he paused while he took in the crossed swords on my cap, said, "Morning, Sarge. I'm the new emergency pilot. I have to report to Captain McNulty."

I knew we were due for another pilot now that Jeff Durkin had been promoted to the snooty Martian scent-bottle *Prometheus*. So this was his successor. He was a Terrestrial all right, but neither black nor white. His expressionless but capable face looked as if covered with old, well-seasoned leather. His eyes held fires resembling phosphorescence. There was an air about him that marked him an exceptional individual the like of which I'd never met before.

"Welcome, Tiny," I offered, getting a crick in the neck as I stared up at him. I did not offer my hand because I wanted it for use later on. "Open your satchel and leave it in the sterilizing chamber. You'll find the skipper in the bow."

"Thanks," he responded without the glimmer of a smile. He stepped into the airlock, hauling the rawhide hay-barn with him.

"We blast in forty minutes," I warned.

Didn't see anything more of Jay Score until we were two hundred thousand out, with Earth a greenish moon at the end of our vapour-trail. Then I heard him in the passage asking someone where he could find the sergeant-at-arms. He was directed through my door.

6

"Sarge," he said, handing over his official requisition, "I've come to collect the trimmings." Then he leaned on the barrier, the whole framework creaked and the top tube sagged in the middle.

"Hey!" I shouted.

"Sorry!" He unleaned. The barrier stood much better when he kept his mass to himself.

Stamping his requisition, I went into the armoury, dug out his needle-ray projector and a box of capsules for same. The biggest Venusian mud-skis I could find were about eleven sizes too small and a yard too short for him, but they'd have to do. I gave him a can of thin, multipurpose oil, a jar of graphite, a Lepanto power-pack for his microwave radiophone and, finally, a bunch of nutweed pellicules marked: "Compliments of the Bridal Planet Aromatic Herb Corporation."

Shoving back the spicy lumps, he said, "You can have 'em—they give me the staggers." The rest of the stuff he forced into his side-pack without so much as twitching an eyebrow. Long time since I'd seen anyone so poker-faced.

All the same, the way he eyed the space-suits seemed strangely wistful. There were thirty bifurcated ones for the Terrestrials, all hanging on the wall like sloughed skins. Also there were six head-and-shoulder helmets for the Martians, since they needed no more than three pounds of air. There wasn't a suit for him. I couldn't have fitted him with one if my life had depended upon it. It'd have been like trying to can an elephant.

Well, he lumbered out lightly, if you get what I mean. The casual, loose-limbed way he transported his tonnage made me think I'd like to be some place else if ever he got on the rampage. Not that I thought him likely to run amok; he was amiable enough though sphinxlike. But I was fascinated by his air of calm assurance and by his motion which was fast, silent and eerie. Maybe the latter was due to his habit of wearing an inch of sponge-rubber under his big dogs.

I kept an interested eye on Jay Score while the Upsy-daisy made good time on her crawl through the void. Yes, I was more than curious about him because his type was a new one on me despite that I've met plenty in my time.

He remained uncommunicative but kind of quietly cordial. His work was smoothly efficient and in every way satisfactory. McNulty took a great fancy to him, though he'd never been one to greet a newcomer with love and kisses.

Three days out, Jay made a major hit with the Martians. As everyone knows, those goggle-eyed, ten-tentacled, half-breathing kibitzers have stuck harder than glue to the Solar System Chess Championship for more than two centuries. Nobody outside of Mars will ever pry them loose. They are nuts about the game and many's the time I've seen a bunch of them go through all the colours of the spectrum in sheer excitement when at last somebody has moved a pawn after thirty minutes of profound cogitation.

One rest-time Jay spent his entire eight hours under three pounds pressure in the starboard airlock. Through the lock's phones came long silences punctuated by wild and shrill twitterings as if he and the Martians were turning the place into a madhouse. At the end of the time we found our tentacled outside-crew exhausted. It turned out that Jay had consented to play Kli Yang and had forced him to a stalemate. Kli had been sixth runner-up in the last solar mêlée, had been beaten only ten times—each time by a brother Martian, of course.

The red-planet gang had a finger on him after that, or I should say a tentacle-tip. Every rest-time they waylaid him and dragged him into the airlock. When we were eleven days out he played the six of them simultaneously, lost two games, stalemated three, won one. They thought he was a veritable whizzbang—for a mere Terrestrial. Knowing their peculiar abilities in this respect, I thought so, too. So did McNulty. He went so far as to enter the sporting data in the log.

You may remember the stunt that the audiopress of 2270 boosted as 'McNulty's Miracle Move'? It's practically a legend of the spaceways. Afterward, when we'd got safely home, McNulty disclaimed the credit and put it where it rightfully belonged. The audiopress had a good excuse, as usual. They said he was the captain, wasn't he? And his name made the headline alliterative, didn't it? Seems that there must be a sect of audio-journalists who have to be alliterative to gain salvation.

What precipitated that crazy stunt and whitened my hair was a chunk of cosmic flotsam. Said object took the form of a gob of meteoric nickel-iron ambling along at the characteristic speed of *pssst!* Its orbit lay on the planetary plane and it approached at right angles to our sunward course.

It gave us the business. I'd never have believed anything so small could have made such a slam. To the present day I can hear the dreadful whistle of air as it made a mad break for freedom through that jagged hole.

We lost quite a bit of political juice before the auto-doors sealed the damaged section. Pressure already had dropped to nine pounds when the compensators held it and slowly began to build it up again. The fall didn't worry the Martians; to them nine pounds was like inhaling pigwash.

There was one engineer in that sealed section. Another escaped the closing doors by the skin of his left ear. But the first, we thought, had drawn his fateful number and eventually would be floated out like so many spacemen who've come to the end of their duty.

The guy who got clear was leaning against a bulwark, white-faced from the narrowness of his squeak. Jay Score came pounding along. His jaw was working, his eyes were like lamps, but his voice was cool and easy.

He said, "Get out. Seal this room. I'll try make a snatch. Open up and let me out fast when I knock."

With that he shoved us from the room which we sealed by closing its autodoor. We couldn't see what the big hunk was doing but the telltale showed he'd released and opened the door to the damaged section. Couple of seconds later the light went out, showing the door had been closed again. Then came a hard, urgent knock. We opened. Jay plunged through with the engineer's limp body cuddled in his huge arms. He bore it as if it were no bigger and heavier than a kitten and the way he took it down the passage threatened to carry him clear through the end of the ship.

Meanwhile we found we were in a first-class mess. The

9

rockets weren't functioning any more. The venturi tubes were okay and the combustion chambers undamaged. The injectors worked without a hitch—provided that they were pumped by hand. We had lost none of our precious fuel and the shell was intact save for that one jagged hole. What made us useless was the wrecking of our co-ordinated feeding and firing controls. They had been located where the big bullet went through and now they were so much scrap.

This was more than serious. General opinion called it certain death though nobody said so openly. I'm pretty certain that McNulty shared the morbid notion even if his official report did under-describe it as "an embarrassing predicament." That is just like McNulty. It's a wonder he didn't define our feelings by recording that we were somewhat nonplussed.

Anyway, the Martian squad poured out, some honest work being required of them for the first time in six trips. Pressure had crawled back to fourteen pounds and they had to come into it to be fitted with their head-and-shoulder contraptions.

Kli Yang sniffed offensively, waved a disgusted tentacle and chirruped, "I could swim!" He eased up when we got his dingbat fixed and exhausted it to his customary three pounds. That is the Martian idea of sarcasm: whenever the atmosphere is thicker than they like they make sinuous backstrokes and declaim, "I could swim!"

To give them their due, they were good. A Martian can cling to polished ice and work continuously for twelve hours on a ration of oxygen that wouldn't satisfy a Terrestrial for more than ninety minutes. I watched them beat it through the airlock, eyes goggling through inverted fishbowls, their tentacles clutching power lines, sealing plates and quasi-arc welders. Blue lights made little auroras outside the ports as they began to cut, shape and close up that ragged hole.

All the time we continued to bullet sunward. But for this accursed misfortune we'd have swung a curve into the orbit of Venus in four hours' time. Then we'd have let her catch us up while we decelerated to a safe landing.

But when that peewee planetoid picked on us we were still heading for the biggest and brightest furnace here-

10

abouts. This was the way we continued to go, our original velocity being steadily increased by the pull of our fiery destination.

I wanted to be cremated—but not yet!

Up in the bow navigation-room Jay Score remained in constant conference with Captain McNulty and the two astro-computator operators. Outside, the Martians continued to crawl around, fizzing and spitting with flashes of ghastly blue light. The engineers, of course, weren't waiting for them to finish their job. Four space-suits entered the wrecked section and started the task of creating order out of chaos.

I envied all those busy guys and so did many others. There's a lot of consolation in being able to do something even in an apparently hopeless situation. There's a lot of misery in being compelled to play with one's fingers while others are active.

Two Martians came back through the lock, grabbed some more sealing-plates and crawled out again. One of them thought it might be a bright idea to take his pocket chess set as well, but I didn't let him. There are times and places for that sort of thing and knight to king's fourth on the skin of a busted boat isn't one of them. Then I went along to see Sam Hignett, our Negro surgeon.

Sam had managed to drag the engineer back from the rim of the grave. He'd done it with oxygen, adrenalin and heart-massage. Only his long, dexterous fingers could have achieved it. It was a feat of surgery that has been brought off before, but not often.

Seemed that Sam didn't know what had happened and didn't much care, either. He was like that when he had a patient on his hands. Deftly he closed the chest incision with silver clips, painted the pinched flesh with iodized plastic, cooled the stuff to immediate hardness with a spray of ether.

"Sam," I told him. "You're a marvel."

"Jay gave me a fair chance," he said. "He got him here in time."

"Why put the blame on him?" I joked, unfunnily.

"Sergeant," he answered, very serious, "I'm the ship's

11

doctor. I do the best I can. I couldn't have saved this man if Jay hadn't brought him when he did."

"All right, all right," I agreed. "Have it your own way."

A good fellow, Sam. But he was like all doctors—you know, ethical. I left him with his feebly breathing patient.

McNulty came strutting along the catwalk as I went back. He checked the fuel tanks. He was doing it personally, and that meant something. He looked worried, and that meant a lot. It meant that I need not bother to write my last will and testament because it would never be read by anything living.

His portly form disappeared into the bow navigation-room and I heard him say, "Jay, I guess you——" before the closing door cut off his voice.

He appeared to have a lot of faith in Jay Score. Well, that individual certainly looked capable enough. The skipper and the new emergency pilot continued to act like cronies even while heading for the final frizzle.

One of the emigrating agriculturalists came out of his cabin and caught me before I regained the armoury. Studying me wide-eyed, he said, "Sergeant, there's a half-moon showing through my port."

He continued to pop them at me while I popped mine at him. Venus showing her half pan meant that we were now crossing her orbit. He knew it too—I could tell by the way he bugged them.

"Well," he persisted, with ill-concealed nervousness, "how long is this mishap likely to delay us?"

"No knowing." I scratched my head, trying to look stupid and confident at one and the same time. "Captain McNulty will do his utmost. Put your trust in him—Poppa knows best."

"You don't think we are ... er ... in any danger?"

"Oh, not at all."

"You're a liar," he said.

"I resent having to admit it," said I.

That unhorsed him. He returned to his cabin, dissatisfied, apprehensive. In short time he'd see Venus in three-quarter phase and would tell the others. Then the fat would be in the fire.

Our fat in the solar fire.

The last vestiges of hope had drained away just about the time when a terrific roar and violent trembling told that the long-dead rockets were back in action. The noise didn't last more than a few seconds. They shut off quickly, the brief burst serving to show that repairs were effective and satisfactory.

The noise brought out the agriculturalist at full gallop. He knew the worst by now and so did the others. It had been impossible to conceal the truth for three days since he'd seen Venus as a half-moon. She was far behind us now. We were cutting the orbit of Mercury. But still the passengers clung to desperate hope that someone would perform an unheard-of miracle.

Charging into the armoury, he yipped, "The rockets are working again. Does that mean——?"

"Nothing," I gave back, seeing no point in building false hopes.

"But can't we turn around and go back?" He mopped perspiration trickling down his jowls. Maybe a little of it was forced out by fear, but most of it was due to the unpleasant fact that interior conditions had become anything but arctic.

"Sir," I said, feeling my shirt sticking to my back, "we've got more pull than any bunch of spacemen ever enjoyed before. And we're moving so fast that there's nothing left to do but hold a lily."

"My ranch," he growled, bitterly. "I've been allotted five thousand acres of the best Venusian tobacco-growing territory, not to mention a range of uplands for beef."

"Sorry, but I think you'll be lucky ever to see it."

Crrrump! went the rockets again. The burst bent me backward and made him bow forward like he had a bad bellyache. Up in the bow, McNulty or Jay Score or someone was blowing them whenever he felt the whim. I couldn't see any sense in it.

"What's that for?" demanded the complainant, regaining the perpendicular.

13

"Boys will be boys," I said.

Snorting his disgust he went to his cabin. A typical Terrestrial emigrant, big, healthy and tough, he was slow to crack and temporarily too peeved to be really worried in any genuinely soul-shaking way.

Half an hour later the general call sounded on buzzers all over the boat. It was a ground signal, never used in space. It meant that the entire crew and all other occupants of the vessel were summoned to the central cabin. Imagine guys being called from their posts in full flight!

Something unique in the history of space navigation must have been behind that call, probably a compose-your-selves-for-the-inevitable-end speech by McNulty.

Expecting the skipper to preside over the last rites, I wasn't surprised to find him standing on the tiny dais as we assembled. A faint scowl lay over his plump features but it changed to a ghost of a smile when the Martians mooched in and one of them did some imitation shark-dodging.

Erect beside McNulty, expressionless as usual, Jay Score looked at that swimming Martian as if he were a pane of glass. Then his strangely lit orbs shifted their aim as if they'd seen nothing more boring. The swim-joke was getting stale, anyway.

"Men and vedras," began McNulty—the latter being the Martian word for 'adults' and, by implication, another piece of Martian sarcasm—"I have no need to enlarge upon the awkwardness of our position." That man certainly could pick his words—awkward! "Already we are nearer the Sun than any vessel has been in the whole history of cosmic navigation."

"Comic navigation," murmured Kli Yang, with tactless wit.

"We'll need your humour to entertain us later," observed Jay Score in a voice so flat that Kli Yang subsided.

"We are moving toward the luminary," went on McNulty, his scowl reappearing, "faster than any ship moved before. Bluntly, there is not more than one chance in ten thousand of us getting out of this alive." He favoured Kli Yang with a challenging stare but that tentacled indi-

14

vidual was now subdued. "However, there is that one chance—and we are going to take it."

We gaped at him, wondering what he meant. Every one of us knew our terrific velocity made it impossible to describe a U-turn and get back without touching the Sun. Neither could we fight our way in the reverse direction with all that mighty drag upon us. There was nothing to do but go onward, onward, until the final searing blast scattered our disrupted molecules.

"What we intend is to try a cometary," continued McNulty. "Jay and myself and the astro-computators think it's remotely possible that we might achieve it and pull through."

That was plain enough. The stunt was a purely theoretical one frequently debated by mathematicians and astro-navigators but never tried out in grim reality. The idea is to build up all the velocity that can be got and at the same time to angle into the path of an elongated, elliptical orbit resembling that of a comet. In theory, the vessel might then skim close to the Sun so supremely fast that it would swing pendulumlike far out to the opposite side of the orbit whence it came. A sweet trick—but could we make it?

"Calculations show our present condition fair enough to permit a small chance of success," said McNulty. "We have power enough and fuel enough to build up the necessary velocity with the aid of the Sun-pull, to strike the necessary angle and to maintain it for the necessary time. The only point about which we have serious doubts is that of whether we can survive at our nearest to the Sun." He wiped perspiration, unconsciously emphasising the shape of things to come. "I won't mince words, men. It's going to be rotten!"

"We'll see it through, skipper," said someone. A low murmur of support sounded through the cabin.

Kli Yang stood up, simultaneously waggled four jointless arms for attention, and twittered, "It is an idea. It is excellent. I, Kli Yang, indorse it on behalf of my fellow vedras. We shall cram ourselves into the refrigerator and suffer the Terrestrial smell while the Sun goes past."

Ignoring that crack about human odour, McNulty

15

nodded and said, "Everybody will be packed into the cold room and endure it as best they can."

"Exactly," said Kli. "Quite," he added with bland disregard of superfluity. Wiggling a tentacle-tip at McNulty, he carried on, "But we cannot control the ship while squatting in the ice-box like three and a half dozen strawberry sundaes. There will have to be a pilot in the bow. One individual can hold her on course—until he gets fried. So somebody has to be the fryee."

He gave the tip another sinuous wiggle being under the delusion that it was fascinating his listeners into complete attention. "And since it cannot be denied that we Martians are far less susceptible to extremes of heat, I suggest that——"

McNulty snapped a harsh remark. His gruffness deceived nobody. The Martians were nuisances—but grand guys.

"All right." Kli's chirrup rose to a shrill, protesting yelp. "Who else is entitled to become a crisp?"

"Me," said Jay Score. It was odd the way he voiced it. Just as if he were a candidate so obvious that only the stone-blind couldn't see him.

He was right, at that! Jay was the very one for the job. If anyone could take what was going to come through the fore observation ports it was Jay Score. He was big and tough, built for just such a task as this. He had a lot of stuff that none of us had got and, after all, he was a fully qualified emergency pilot. And most definitely this was an emergency, the greatest ever.

But it was funny the way I felt about him. I could imagine him up in front, all alone, nobody there, our lives depending on how much he could take, while the tremendous Sun extended its searing fingers——

"You!" snapped Kli Yang, breaking my train of thought. His goggle eyes bulged irefully at the big, laconic figure on the dais. "You would! I am ready to mate in four moves, as you are miserably aware, and promptly you scheme to lock yourself away."

"Six moves," contradicted Jay, airily. "You cannot do it in less than six."

"Four!" Kli Yang fairly howled. "And right at this point you——"

It was too much for the listening McNulty. He looked as if on the verge of a stroke. His purple face turned to the semaphoring Kli.

"Forget your blasted chess!" he roared. "Return to your stations, all of you. Make ready for maximum boost. I will sound the general call immediately it becomes necessary to take cover and then you will all go to the cold room." He started around, the purple gradually fading as his blood pressure went down. "That is, everyone except Jay."

More like old times with the rockets going full belt. They thundered smoothly and steadily. Inside the vessel the atmosphere became hotter and hotter until moisture trickled continually down our backs and a steaminess lay over the gloss of the walls. What it was like in the bow navigation-room I didn't know and didn't care to discover. The Martians were not incovenienced yet; for once their whacky composition was much to be envied.

I did not keep check on the time but I'd had two spells of duty with one intervening sleep period before the buzzers gave the general call. By then things had become bad. I was no longer sweating: I was slowly melting into my boots.

Sam, of course, endured it most easily of all the Terrestrials and had persisted long enough to drag his patient completely out of original danger. That engineer was lucky, if it's lucky to be saved for a bonfire. We put him in the cold room right away, with Sam in attendance.

The rest of us followed when the buzzer went. Our sanctuary was more than a mere refrigerator; it was the strongest and coolest section of the vessel, a heavily armoured, triple shielded compartment holding the instrument lockers, two sick bays and a large lounge for the benefit of space-nauseated passengers. It held all of us comfortably.

All but the Martians. It held them, but not comfortably. They are never comfortable at fourteen pounds pressure which they regard as not only thick but also smelly—something like breathing molasses impregnated with aged goat.

17

Under our very eyes Kli Yang produced a bottle of *hooloo* scent, handed it to his half-parent Kli Morg. The latter took it, stared at us distastefully then sniffed the bottle in an ostentatious manner that was positively insulting. But nobody said anything.

All were present excepting McNulty and Jay Score. The skipper appeared two hours later. Things must have been raw up front, for he looked terrible. His haggard face was beaded and glossy, his once-plump cheeks sunken and blistered. His usually spruce, well-fitting uniform hung upon him sloppily. It needed only one glance to tell that he'd had a darned good roasting, as much as he could stand.

Walking unsteadily, he crossed the floor, went into the first-aid cubby, stripped himself with slow, painful movements. Sam rubbed him with tannic jelly. We could hear the tormented skipper grunting hoarsely as Sam put plenty of pep into the job.

The heat was now on us with a vengeance. It pervaded the walls, the floor, the air and created a multitude of fierce stinging sensations in every muscle of my body. Several of the engineers took off their boots and jerkins. In short time the passengers followed suit, discarding most of their outer clothing. My agriculturalist sat a miserable figure in tropical silks, moody over what might have been.

Emerging from the cubby, McNulty flopped into a bunk and said, "If we're all okay in four hours' time, we're through the worst part."

At that moment the rockets faltered. We knew at once what was wrong. A fuel tank had emptied and a relay had failed to cut in. An engineer should have been standing by to switch the conduits. In the heat and excitement, someone had blundered.

The fact barely had time to register before Kli Yang was out through the door. He'd been lolling nearest to it and was gone while we were trying to collect our overheated wits. Twenty seconds later the rockets renewed their steady thrum.

An intercom bell clanged right by my ear. Switching its mike, I croaked a throaty, "Well?" and heard Jay's voice coming back at me from the bow.

"Who did it?"

"Kli Yang," I told him. "He's still outside."

"Probably gone for their domes," guessed Jay. "Tell him I said thanks."

"What's it like around where you live?" I asked.

"Fierce. It isn't so good . . . for vision." Silence a moment, then, "Guess I can stick it . . . somehow. Strap down or hold on ready for next time I sound the . . . bell."

"Why?" I half yelled, half rasped.

"Going to rotate her. Try . . . distribute . . . the heat."

A faint squeak told that he'd switched off. I told the others to strap down. The Martians didn't have to bother about that because they owned enough saucer-sized suckers to weld them to a sunfishing meteor.

Kli came back, showed Jay's guess to be correct; he was dragging the squad's head-and-shoulder pieces. The load was as much as he could pull now that temperature had climbed to the point where even he began to wilt.

The Martian moochers gladly donned their gadgets, sealing the seams and evacuating them down to three pounds pressure. It made them considerably happier. Remembering that we Terrestrials use spacesuits to keep air inside, it seemed peculiar to watch those guys using theirs to keep it outside.

They had just finished making themselves comfortable and had laid out a chessboard in readiness for a minor tourney when the bell sounded again. We braced ourselves. The Martians clamped down their suckers.

Slowly and steadily the *Upsydaisy* began to turn upon her longitudinal axis. The chessboard and pieces tried to stay put, failed, crawled along the floor, up the wall and across the ceiling. Solar pull was making them stick to the sunward side.

I saw Kli Morg's strained, heat-ridden features glooming at a black bishop while it skittered around, and I suppose that inside his goldfish bowl were resounding some potent samples of Martian invective.

"Three hours and a half," gasped McNulty.

That four hours estimate could only mean two hours of approach to the absolute deadline and two hours of retreat from it. So the moment when we had two hours to go would be the moment when we were at our nearest to the solar furnace, the moment of greatest peril.

I wasn't aware of that critical time, since I passed out twenty minutes before it arrived. No use enlarging upon the horror of that time. I think I went slightly nuts. I was a hog in an oven, being roasted alive. It's the only time I've ever thought the Sun ought to be extinguished for keeps. Soon afterward I became incapable of any thought at all.

I recovered consciousness and painfully moved in my straps ninety minutes after passing the midway point. My dazed mind had difficulty in realizing that we had now only half an hour to go to reach theoretical safety.

What had happened in the interim was left to my imagination and I didn't care to try picture it just then. The Sun blazing with a ferocity multi-million times greater than that of a tiger's eye, and a hundred thousand times as hungry for our blood and bones. The flaming corona licking out toward this shipload of half-dead entities, imprisoned in a steel bottle.

And up in front of the vessel, behind its totally inadequate quartz observation-ports, Jay Score sitting alone, facing the mounting inferno, staring, staring, staring——

Getting to my feet I teetered uncertainly, went down like a bundle of rags. The ship wasn't rotating any longer and we appeared to be bulleting along in normal fashion. What dropped me was sheer weakness. I felt lousy.

The Martians already had recovered. I knew they'd be the first. One of them lugged me upright and held me steady while I regained a percentage of my former control. I noticed that another had sprawled right across the unconscious McNulty and three of the passengers. Yes, he'd shielded them from some of the heat and they were the next ones to come to life.

Struggling to the intercom, I switched it but got no response from the front. For three full minutes I hung by it dazedly before I tried again. Nothing doing. Jay wouldn't or couldn't answer.

I was stubborn about it, made several more attempts with no better result. The effort cost me a dizzy spell and down I flopped once more. The heat was still terrific. I

20

felt more dehydrated than a mummy dug out of sand a million years old.

Kli Yang opened the door, crept out with dragging, pain-stricken motion. His air-helmet was secure on his shoulders. Five minutes later he came back, spoke through the helmet's diaphragm.

"Couldn't get near the bow navigation-room. At the midway catwalk the autodoors are closed, the atmosphere sealed off and it's like being inside a furnace." He stared around, met my gaze, answered the question in my eyes. "There's no air in the bow."

No air meant the observation-ports had gone *phut*. Nothing else could have emptied the navigation-room. Well, we carried spares for that job and could make good the damage once we got into the clear. Meanwhile here we were roaring along, maybe on correct course and maybe not, with an empty, airless navigation-room and with an intercom system that gave nothing but ghastly silence.

Sitting around we picked up strength. The last to come out of his coma was the sick engineer. Sam brought him through again. It was about then that McNulty wiped sweat, showed sudden excitement.

"Four hours, men," he said, with grim satisfaction. "We've done it!"

We raised a hollow cheer. By Jupiter, the superheated atmosphere seemed to grow ten degrees cooler with the news. Strange how relief from tension can breed strength; in one minute we had conquered former weakness and were ready to go. But it was yet another four hours before a quartet of spacesuited engineers penetrated the forward hell and bore their burden from the airless navigation-room.

They carried him into Sam's cubby-hole, a long, heavy, silent figure with face burned black.

Stupidly I hung around him saying, "Jay, Jay, how're you making out?"

He must have heard, for he moved the fingers of his right hand and emitted a chesty, grinding noise. Two of the engineers went to his cabin, brought back his huge

21

rawhide case. They shut the door, staying in with Sam and leaving me and the Martians fidgeting outside. Kli Yang wandered up and down the passage as if he didn't know what to do with his tentacles.

Sam came out after more than an hour. We jumped him on the spot.

"How's Jay?"

"Blind as a statue." He shook his woolly head. "And his voice isn't there any more. He's taken an awful beating."

"So that's why he didn't answer the intercom." I looked him straight in the eyes. "Can you . . . can you do anything for him, Sam?"

"I only wish I could." His sepia face showed his feelings. "You know how much I'd like to put him right. But I can't." He made a gesture of futility. "He is completely beyond my modest skill. Nobody less than Johannsen can help him. Maybe when we get back to Earth——" His voice petered out and he went back inside.

Klu Yang said, miserably, "I am saddened."

A scene I'll never forget to my dying day was that evening we spent as guests of the Astro Club in New York. That club was then—as it is today—the most exclusive group of human beings ever gathered together. To qualify for membership one had to perform in dire emergency a feat of astro-navigation tantamount to a miracle. There were nine members in those days and there are only twelve now.

Mace Waldron, the famous pilot who saved that Martian liner in 2263, was the chairman. Classy in his soup and fish, he stood at the top of the table with Jay Score sitting at his side. At the opposite end of the table was McNulty, a broad smirk of satisfaction upon his plump pan. Beside the skipper was old, white-haired Knud Johannsen, the genius who designed the J-series and a scientific figure known to every spaceman.

Along the sides, manifestly self-conscious, sat the entire crew of the *Upsydaisy*, including the Martians, plus three of our passengers who'd postponed their trips for this occasion. There were also a couple of audio-journalists with scanners and mikes.

"Gentlemen and vedras," said Mace Waldron, "this is an event without precedent in the history of humanity, an event never thought-of, never imagined by this club. Because of that I feel it doubly an honour and a privilege to propose that Jay Score, Emergency Pilot, be accepted as a fully qualified and worthy member of the Astro Club."

"Seconded!" shouted three members simultaneously.

"Thank you, gentlemen." He cocked an inquiring eyebrow. Eight hands went up in unison. "Carried," he said. "Unanimously." Glancing down at the taciturn and unmoved Jay Score, he launched into a eulogy. It went on and on and on, full of praise and superlatives, while Jay squatted beside him with a listless air.

Down at the other end I saw McNulty's gratified smirk grow stronger and stronger. Next to him, old Knud was gazing at Jay with a fatherly fondness that verged on the fatuous. The crew likewise gave full attention to the blank-faced subject of the talk, and the scanners were fixed upon him too.

I returned my attention to where all the others were looking, and the victim sat there, his restored eyes bright and glittering, but his face completely immobile despite the talk, the publicity, the beam of paternal pride from Johannsen.

But after ten minutes of this I saw J.20 begin to fidget with obvious embarrassment.

Don't let anyone tell you that a robot can't have feelings!

MECHANISTRIA

There we were, standing on the mezzanine of Terrastro-port Seven Administration Building. Not a darned one of us knew why we had been summoned so unexpectedly or why we weren't blasting as usual for Venus in the morning.

So we hung around, asking unanswerable questions of each other with our eyes and getting ourselves nowhere. I had once seen thirty Venusian guppies gaping in adenoidal dumbfoundment at an Aberdeen terrier named Fergus and straining their peanut brains for the reason why one end waggled. They looked pretty much as we were looking right now.

Portly and bland as ever, Captain McNulty came along just as the nail-gnawing contest was about to begin. He was followed by half a dozen of the *Upsydaisy's* leading technicians and a skinny little runt we'd never seen before.

In the rear came Jay Score walking lithely over floorboards that squeaked under his three hundred or more pounds. I never failed to be surprised by the casual ease with which he bore his massive frame. His eyes were aglow as they gave us that all-embracing look.

Gesturing to us to follow, McNulty led us into a room, strutted onto its small platform and addressed us in the manner of one about to tutor a newly-formed third grade.

"Gentlemen and vedras, I have with me this afternoon the famous Professor Flettner."

He made a precise bow toward the runt who grinned and did a bit of foot-twisting like a kid caught snitching the fudge.

"The professor is seeking a crew for his extra-solarian

24

vessel, the *Marathon*. Jay Score and six of our technicians have volunteered to go along with me. We have been accepted and have received the necessary extra training during the term of your leave."

"It was a pleasure," put in Flettner, anxious to placate us for stealing the skipper.

"The Terrestrial Government," continued McNulty, flattered, "has approved the entire complement of my former command, the Venusian freighter *Upskadaska City*. Now it's up to you fellows. Those who may wish to stay with the *Upskadaska City* can leave this meeting and report for duty. Will those who prefer to accompany me please signify by raising a hand." Then his roving eye discovered the Martians and he hastily added, "Or a tentacle."

Sam Hignett promptly stuck up his brown mitt. "Captain, I'd rather stay with you."

He beat the rest of us by a fraction of a second. Funny thing, not a single one of us was really bursting to shoot around in Flettner's suicide-box. It was merely that we were too weak to refuse. Or maybe we stuck out our necks for the sake of seeing the look that came into McNulty's features.

"Thank you, men," said McNulty in the solemn sort of voice they use at burials. He swallowed hard, blew his nose. His gaze roamed over us almost lovingly, became suddenly abashed as it discovered one Martian figure flopped in a corner, all its limp tentacles sprawling negligently around.

"Why, Sug Farn——" he began.

Kli Yang, chief coach of the Red Planet bunch, chipped in quickly with "I put up two tentacles, Captain. One for myself and one for him. He is asleep. He deputed me to act on his behalf, to say yes, or say no, or sing, 'Pop Goes the Weasel' as required."

Everyone laughed. Sug Farn's utter and complete laziness had been a feature of life aboard the *Upsydaisy*. The skipper alone was unaware that nothing short of an urgent outside job or a game of chess could keep Sug Farn awake. Our laughter ended and the sleeper immediately filled in the silence with one of those eerie, high-pitched whistles that is the Martian version of a snore.

"All right," said McNulty, striving to keep a smile away from his mouth. "I want you to report aboard ship at dawn. We blast at ten ack emma G.M.T. I'll leave Jay Score to give you further information and answer any questions."

The *Marathon* was a real beauty, Flettner designed, government built, with fine lines halfway between those of a war cruiser and those of a light racing rocket. Indeed, she had space-navy fittings that were luxurious by comparison with what we'd had on the *Upsydaisy*. I liked her a lot. So did the rest.

Standing at the top of the telescopic metal gangway, I watched the last comers arrive. Jay Score went down, returned lugging his enormous case. He was allowed more weight in personal luggage than any three others. No wonder, for only one item among his belongings was a spare atomic engine, a lovely little piece of engineering coming to eighty pounds. In a way, this was his standby heart.

Four government experts came aboard in a bunch. I'd no idea of who they were or why they were going with us, but directed them to their private cabins. The last arrival was young Wilson, a fair-haired, moody lad of about nineteen. He'd had three boxes delivered in advance and now was trying to drag three more aboard.

"What's in those?" I demanded.

"Plates." He surveyed the ship with unconcealed distaste.

"Repair, dinner or dental?" I inquired.

"Photographic," he snapped without a glimmer of a smile.

"You the official picture man?"

"Yes."

"All right. Dump those boxes in mid-hold."

He scowled. "They are never dumped, dropped, chucked or slung. They are placed," he said. "Gently."

"You heard me!" I liked the kid's looks but not his surly attitude.

Putting down the boxes at the top of the gangway, and doing it with exaggerated care, he looked me over very slowly, his gaze travelling from feet to head and all the way down again. His lips were thin, his knuckles white.

Then he said, "And who might you be when you're outside your shirt?"

"I'm the sergeant-at-arms," I informed in I'm-having-no-nonsense-from-you tones. "Now go dump or place or lower those crates someplace where they'll be safe, else I'll toss them a hundred feet Earthward."

That got him right in his weak spot. I think that if I'd threatened to throw him for a loop he'd have had a try at giving me an orbit of my own. But he didn't intend to let me or anyone else pick on his precious boxes.

Favouring me with a glance that promised battle, murder and sudden death, he carried the boxes into midhold, taking them one at a time, tenderly, as if they were babies. That was the last I saw of him for a while. I had been hard on the kid but didn't realize it at the time.

A couple of the passengers were arguing in their harness just before we threw ourselves away. Part of my job is to inspect the strappings of novices and they kept at it while I was going over their belts and buckles.

"Say what you like," offered one, "but it works, doesn't it?"

"I know it does," snorted the other, showing irritation. "That's just it. I've been right through Flettner's crazy mathematics a thousand times, until my mind's dizzy with symbols. The logic is all right. It's unassailable. Nevertheless, the premise is completely cockeyed."

"So what? His first two ships reached the Jovian system simply by going *zip!* and *zip!* They did the round trip in less time than any ordinary rocketship takes to make up its mind to boost. Is that crazy?"

"It's blatantly nuts!" swore the objector, his blood pressure continuing to rise. "It's magic and it's nuts! Flettner says all astronomical estimates of distances can be scrapped and thrown into the ash-can because there's no such thing as speed inside a cosmos which itself plasma and ether alike is in a series of tremendous motions of infinite variability. He says you can't have speed or measurable velocity where there's nothing to which you can relate it except a fixed point which is purely imaginary and cannot possibly exist. He claims that we're obsessed by speeds and distances because our minds are conditioned by established relations inside our own one-cent solar system, but in the greater cosmos there are no limitations to which our inadequate yardstick can be applied."

"Me," I put in soothingly, "I've made my last will and testament."

He glared at me, then snapped to the other, "I still say it's looney."

"So's television and arguers," retorted his opponent, "but they both work."

McNulty came by the door at that moment, paused, said, "Seen to that lad Wilson yet?"

"No—I'll be there in one minute."

"Try and cool him down, will you. He looks as if he's in a blue funk."

Reaching Wilson's cabin, I found him sitting there with his harness on. He was dumb, glassy-eyed and worried stiff.

"Ever been on a spaceship before?"

"No," he growled.

"Well, don't let it bother you. I admit there are rare occasions when people go up in one piece and come down in several, but according to official statistics the roller coasters killed more last year."

"Do you think I'm scared?" he demanded, standing up so quickly that he startled me.

"Me? Oh, no!" I fumbled around for words I couldn't find. His bothered expression had vanished and he was looking rather hard. "See here," I said, speaking as man to man, "tell me what's eating you and I'll see if I can help."

"You can't help." Sitting down, he relaxed, became as moody as before. "I'm worrying about my plates."

"What plates?"

"Those photographic ones I brought on board, of course."

"Heck, they'll be safe enough. Besides, what good will worrying do?"

"Plenty," he said. "When at first I let 'em go on trust I had them walloped to powder in two successive accidents. Then I developed the habit of worrying about them. I was doing a really good job of worrying just before that Century Express smashup and I lost only two, both unexposed. I worried all but six of my outfit through the big Naples quake. So it pays me, see? Leave me alone and let me get on with my job," he invited. Upon which he leaned backward, tightened his harness and calmly resumed his worrying.

Can you tie that? I was still stupefied by the queer tricks of some professions when I arrived at the scene of the uproar at the top of the starboard gangway. McNulty was bawling out the Martians. The latter had emerged from their especial quarters where air was kept down to the three pounds pressure to which they were accustomed. They were now outside in the alien and objectionable atmosphere.

Somebody went solemnly down the gangway bearing Earthward an enormous vase of violently clashing colours and exceedingly repulsive shape. The Martian chorus of protest arose crescendo. There were shrill chirrups and much snaking of angry tentacles. I gathered that the porcelain monstrosity was Kli Morg's chess trophy, the Martian notion of a championship cup. It was in vile taste from the Terrestrial viewpoint. Anyway, the skipper's orders were orders and the abomination stayed on Earth.

Next instant the siren howled its thirty seconds warning and all those still out of harness raced for safety. The way those Martians ceased their oratory and beat it was something worth seeing.

I got myself fixed in the nick of time. The air-locks closed. *Whooom!* A giant hand tried to force my cranium down into my boots and temporarily I passed out.

The world swelling rapidly before our bow was little bigger than Terra. Its sunlit face had a mixture of blacks, reds and silvers rather than the old familiar browns, blues and greens. It was one of five planets circling a sun smaller and whiter than our own. A small, insignificant group of asteroids shared this grouping but we had no difficulty in cutting through their orbits.

I don't know which star that sun was supposed to be. Jay Score told me it was a minor luminary in the region of Boötes. We had picked on it because it was the only one in this area with a planetary family and we'd selected the second planet because its present position stood in nice, convenient relationship with our line of flight.

At that, we were going a lot too fast to circle it and submit it to close inspection before landing in some choice spot. We were striking its orbit at a tangent with the planet immediately ahead. The landing was to be a direct one, a hawklike dive with a muffled prayer and no prancing around the mulberry bush.

The way Flettner's unorthodox notions went into action was again something to bring one's heart into one's gullet before it could be swallowed back. I believe that the vessel could have done even better had its functioning not been handicapped by the limits of human endurance. McNulty must have gained the measure of those limits with astonishing accuracy, for the deceleration and drop brought me down alive and kicking—but I had the deep impression of my harness all over my abused carcass for a week.

Reports from the lab said the air was twelve pounds and breathable. We drew lots for first out. McNulty and all the government experts lost. That was a laugh! Kli Yang's name came first out of the hat, then an engineer named Brennand was lucky, followed by Jay Score, Sam Hignett and me.

One hour was our limit. That meant we couldn't go much more than a couple of miles from the *Marathon*. Spacesuits weren't needed. Kli Yang could have used his head-and-shoulder contraption to enjoy his customary three pounds pressure but he decided that he could tolerate twelve for a mere hour without becoming surly. Hanging binoculars around our necks, we strapped on needle-ray guns. Jay Score grabbed a tiny two-way radiophone to keep us in touch with the vessel.

"No fooling, men," warned the skipper as we went through the air-lock. "See all you can and be back within the hour."

Kli Yang, last through the lock, ran his saucer eyes over the envious ship's company, said, "Somebody had better go wake Sug Farn and tell him the fleet's in port." Then four of his ten tentacles released their hold and he dropped to ground.

My, was that alien surface hard! Here it shone black and glassy, there it was silvery and metallic with patches of deep crimson appearing in odd places. I picked up a small lump of silvery outcrop, found it amazingly heavy; solid metal as far as I could tell.

I tossed the lump through the open door of the air-lock so that they could get busy analysing it, and at once Kli Morg stuck out a furious head, goggled his eyes at the inoffensive Kli Yang and remarked, "A blow on the cranium is not funny. The fact that you are now with a bunch of Terrestrials doesn't mean that you have to be equally childish."

"Why, you amateur pawn-pusher," began Kli Yang, speaking with considerable warmth. "I'd have you know ——"

"Shut up!" snapped Jay Score authoritatively. He started off toward the setting sun, his long, agile legs working as though intent on circumnavigating the globe. The radio swung easily from one powerful hand.

We followed in single file. In ten minutes he was half a mile ahead and waiting for us to catch up.

"Remember, long brother, we're only flesh and blood," complained Brennand as we reached the emergency pilot's huge, efficient figure.

"Not me," denied Kli Yang. "Thank Rava, my kind are not made of so sickening a mess." He emitted a thin whistle of disgust, made swimming motions with his tentacles through air four times as thick as that of Mars. "I could row a boat!"

Our progress was slightly slower after that. Down into a deep, shadowy valley, up the other side and over the crest. No trees, no shrubs, no birds, no other sign of life. Nothing but the black, silver and red semimetallic ground, a range of blue veiled mountains in the far distance and the gleaming cylinder of the *Marathon* behind us.

A swiftly flowing river ran down the centre of the next valley. Reaching it, we filled a flask to take back to the lab. Sam Hignett risked a taste, said it was coppery but drinkable. The rushing waters were faintly blue with darker shades swirling in their depths. The banks were of ground considerably softer than the surface we'd just traversed.

Sitting on the nearer bank, we contemplated the torrent which was much too swift and deep to cross. After a while a headless body came floating and bobbing along.

The mutilated corpse vaguely resembled that of an enormous lobster. It had a hard, crimson, chitinous shell, four crablike legs, two lobsterish pincers and was half as big again as a man. Its neck was a raw, bloodless gash from which white strings dangled. What the missing head had looked like we could only imagine.

Full of mute menace, the cadaver turned and rolled past while we sat in a fascinated row and watched it, our eyes going from right to left and following it until it swept round the distant bend. What filled our minds was not the question of how the head looked, but who had removed it and for what reason. Nobody said anything.

This gruesome sight had barely departed in the grip of the rapid current when we got first evidence of life. Ten yards to my right a hole showed in the soft bank. A creature slithered out of it, went to the brink of the water, drank in delicate sips.

Four-legged, with a long triangular tail, it resembled an iguana more than anything else. Its skin was black with an underlying sheen of silver like shot silk. Its pupils were shiny black slots in silvery eyeballs. Length: about six feet, including tail.

Having swallowed its fill, this thing turned round to go back, saw us and stopped abruptly. I fingered my needle-ray just in case it had combative ideas. It examined us carefully, opened its jaws in a wide gape that revealed a great, jet-black gullet and double rows of equally black teeth. Several times it favoured us with this demonstration of biting ability before it made up its mind what to do next. Then, so help me, it crept up the bank, joined the end of our row, sat down and stared at the river.

I have never seen a crazier spectacle than we must

have presented at that moment. There was Jay Score, huge and shining, his craggy features the colour of ancient leather. Next, Sam Hignett, our Negro surgeon, his teeth gleaming in bright contrast with his ebon features. Then Brennand, an undersized white Terrestrial sitting beside Kli Yang, a rubber-skinned ten-tentacled, goggle-eyed Martian. Next, me, a middle-aged, greying Terrestrial and, finally, this black and silver alien wottizit. All of us glumly contemplating the river.

Still nobody said anything. There didn't seem anything adequate to say. We stared, the creature stared, all of us as phlegmatic as could be. I thought of young Wilson and how preciously he'd have mothered a plate with this scene on it. Pity he wasn't there to record it for all time. Then as we watched another body came floating down, one like the first. No head.

"Somebody can't be popular," remarked Brennand, fed up with the silence.

"They're independent," informed the iguana, solemnly. "Like me."

"Eh?"

Five people never stood up with greater promptitude or timed an ejaculation so perfectly.

"Stick around," advised the lizard. "Maybe you'll see something." It blinked at Brennand, then slithered back into its hole. Silver gleamed along its black tail as it went down.

"Well," said Brennand, breathing heavily, "can you pin your ears to that!" A dazed look in his eyes, he went to the hole, squatted on his heels and bawled, "Hey!"

"He isn't in," responded the thing from somewhere in the depths.

Licking his lips, Brennand gave us the piteous glance of a hurt spaniel, then inquired somewhat insanely, "*Who* isn't in?"

"Me," said the lizard.

"Did you hear what I heard?" demanded the flabbergasted Brennand, standing up and staring at us.

"You heard nothing," put in Jay Score before any of us could reply. "It didn't speak. I was watching it closely and its mouth never moved." His hard, brilliant eyes looked into the hole. "It was thinking purely animal

33

thoughts which you received telepathically and, of couse, translated into human terms. But because you are not normally receptive of telepathic thought-forms, and because you have not previously encountered anything that broadcasts on the human waveband, you thought you heard it talking."

"Stick around," repeated the lizard. "But not around my burrow. I don't like the publicity. It's dangerous."

Moving away, Jay picked up the radiophone. "I'll tell them about the bodies and ask if we can explore a mile or two upstream."

He moved a switch. The instrument promptly emitted a noise like Niagara in full flow. Nothing else could be heard. Changing to transmission, he called repeatedly, switched back and was rewarded only by the sound of a mighty waterfall.

"Static," suggested Sam Hignett. "Try lower down the band."

The radio had only a limited bandwidth but Jay turned all the way across it. The waterfall faded out, was gradually replaced by an eerie, dithering sound like that of a million grasshoppers yelling *bitter-bitter-bitter*. That gave way to a high, piercing whistle followed by another waterfall.

"I don't like this," commented Jay, switching off. "There is far too much on the air for what looks like an empty world. We are going back. Come on—let's move fast."

Lifting the radiophone he trudged rapidly up the bank and over the crest. His mighty figure looked like that of some old-time giant as it became silhouetted against the evening sky.

He put on the pace, making it a gruelling task to keep up with him. We needed no urging. Much of his uneasiness had communicated itself to us. Those decapitated bodies——

McNulty heard us through, sent for Steve Gregory and asked him to give the ether a whirl. Steve beat it to the radio room, came back in a few minutes. His eyebrows were tangled.

"Skipper, it's alive from two hundred metres right down into the ultra-short waveband. There isn't room to get a word in edgeways."

"Well," growled McNulty, "what sort of stuff is it?"

"Three kinds," replied Steve. "There are whistles of a steady and sustained type that might be direction signals. There are eight different waterfalls of considerable intensity. I reckon they are power broadcasts. In between all these is an orgy of gabbling which suggests this place is fairly crawling with life." He did more acrobatics with his eyebrows which were of the bushy sort suitable for such performances. "Couldn't get any vision except for typical interference patterns racing across the screen."

Looking apprehensively through the nearest port, one of the government experts opined, "If this planet is well populated we must have picked on the local Sahara."

"We'll use a lifeboat," decided McNulty. "We'll send out three men, well armed, and give them half an hour to look round. They should be able to cover best part of five hundred miles and be back before dark."

Most of us would have liked another lucky dip in the hat, but McNulty nominated the three. One of them was a government biologist named Haines; the others were engineers holding lifeboat coxswain's certificates.

It took no more than four minutes to swing out a lifeboat on its automatic derricks and lower it to ground. The three clambered in. All had needle-ray guns. In addition there were half a dozen miniature atomic bombs on board, while a multiple pom-pom stuck its menacing bunch of barrels through a glassite turret in the tiny vessel's bow.

That little expedition was adequately armed all right! It wasn't so much that we really expected trouble or were going looking for it, but rather that we believed in doing more than keeping our fingers crossed.

With an amusingly squeaky blast the twelve-ton cylinder shot from the *Marathon's* mothering bulk and curved skyward. It whined away to a pinpoint in no time, then it was gone.

Steve had reset the lifeboat's radiophone and now was in touch with it on four-twenty metres. Biologist Haines was at the vessel's observation window doing the reporting.

"Sixty miles out and six miles up. Mountains ahead. We're climbing." Silence for a minute, then, "Over the top at twelve miles altitude. There's a long, straight, artificial-

35

looking line cutting the foothills on the other side. We are diving towards it, lower, lower . . . yes, it's a road!"

"Anything using it?" yelped Steve, his brow-bushes snaking around.

"Nothing as far as we can see just yet. It's in excellent condition. Not deserted, but seldom used. Ah, another road over on the horizon, maybe forty miles away. We're making for it now. Seems as if . . . as if . . . there are shapes moving swiftly along it." Another pause while his listeners danced with impatience. "By heavens, there are dozens——"

The voice blanked out completely. Nothing more came over the ether except a steady rustling noise like that of dead leaves dancing in a random wind.

Frantically, Steve went over his receiver, adjusting, retuning, doing all he knew to bring back the voice so suddenly gone from the air. But there was nothing, nothing except that persistent and eerie whispering on four-twenty and the all-pervading uproar below two hundred.

The crew clamoured for the chance to take out a second boat. We had four of the little vessels as well as the slightly larger and much faster pinnace. McNulty refused to let any more go.

"No, men," he said, his plump features unworried. "One bunch at a time is enough. The rest of us will wait here. We'll stay put until morning to give that boat a chance to find us again. It may be safe enough. Perhaps its radio has gone out of commission or some minor fault has developed among its navigational instruments." A glint came into his eyes. "But if it's not back by dawn we're going to discover the reason why."

"You bet!" came a murmur of many voices.

Thrum-thrum-thrum! The sound had a chance to be noticed during ensuing quietness. We now realized that it had been drumming dully through the room for most of a minute but only then did it register in our minds. A strange yet familiar sound, that steady thrumming—and it wasn't caused by the returning lifeboat.

A crew never poured through the airlock as quickly as we did at that moment. Outside we stood with our backs to the great curved shell of the *Marathon* and stared at the

36

sky. There they were, three, four, five of them: long, black rocketships flying in arrowhead formation.

Young Wilson's face lit up, he yipped, "Oh, lordy!" and produced a camera from nowhere. He sighted it at the black things above.

None of us had been quick-witted enough to bring out binoculars, but Jay Score didn't need any. He stood with his head tilted back, his big chest protruding, his head tilted back, his gleaming orbs focused on the overhead spectacle.

"Five," he said. "Ten miles up, moving fast and still ascending. Either they're painted dead black or made of some very black metal. Don't resemble any design on Terra. Their stern tubes are exposed instead of being sunk in the tail, and they've even got fore and aft fins."

He continued to watch long after I had developed a crick in the neck. Still thrumming faintly, the five disappeared from sight. They had passed right over the *Marathon* without noticing it, blasting at an altitude that made our reposing vessel less conspicuous than a dropped pin.

Kli Morg chirruped, "They're not so far behind us after all. They've got rocketships, they decapitate lobsters, and in all probability they're instinctively hostile towards strangers. I can see them offering us a big tentacle, yes, right in the masticatory orifice!"

"Hope for the best rather than expect the worst," advised McNulty. He gazed around at his crew, then at the sleek shape of the *Marathon*. "Besides, we're a lot faster than anything limited to a mere solar system and we know how to take care of ourselves."

He patted his needle-ray significantly. I'd never seen our plump and amiable skipper look so tough. He had a most disarming habit of understating his sentiments but, at the right time and in the right place, he could be a very hard egg.

Nobody though could look half as tough as Jay Score who was standing at his side. There was something about that guy's firm, solid, statuesque pose, his brief speeches and rapid decisions, and the fiery eyes glowing in a rocklike face, that gave him an appearance of serene power such as you see on the phlegmatic features of those unknown gods they dig out of strange and lonely places.

Jay rumbled, "All right, let's go in and wait for dawn."

"Sure," McNulty agreed. "Tomorrow we'll get some of these mysteries sewed up, whether that boat returns or not."

He didn't know that tomorrow he'd be sewn up himself along with the rest of us. Neither did any of us suspect it. Young Wilson wouldn't have whistled half so shrilly and happily as he developed his exposed plate had he guessed that it would be lost forever within twenty-four hours.

One of the navigators on night watch first saw the machines. They appeared suddenly and furtively about an hour before the pale dawn, ghostly shapes skittering around under dying stars and among the darkest shadows.

At first he thought they were animals of some kind, probably nocturnal carnivores. But his doubts grew too strong, he sounded the general alarm and we dashed to our posts. An engineer trundled a portable searchlight to one of the ports, let its powerful beam probe encompassing gloom.

At the other end of the beam something big and glittering promptly skedaddled out of the cone of light. Its evasive action was so swift that nobody got more than a glimpse of it, a vague, uncertain impression of a tentacled globe encircled in the vertical plane by a rim like that of a wheel. It seemed to roll on this rim, twisting and turning with astounding agility.

The searchlight could not follow it since the beam was pouring through the glassite pane and had no room to sweep sidewise. We waited awhile, tense, expectant, but nothing else trespassed into the bar of revealing brillance, though we could sense many things moving around just beyond reach of the rays.

Digging out a couple more searchlights, we positioned them behind two other ports, tried to catch our beseigers napping by switching the beams on and off at erratic intervals. This method was more effective. Again we caught a momentary view of the dodging globe-thing as it shot away from the sudden lance of the third light.

A minute later the second light illuminated a great, trellis-patterned metal arm as it swung ponderously upward into concealing darkness. There was something big and brutal at the end of that arm, and it wasn't a hand. The thing reminded me of a mechanical excavator or steam-shovel.

"See that?" bawled Steve. His face was shadowed be-behind the searchlights but I knew where his eyebrows were going. Rumour had it they'd once gone right over the top and halfway down his back.

I could hear Brennand breathing heavily beside me, and a faint, subtle hum coming from Jay Score farther up the passage. The searchlights exuded a smell of warm air and warmer metal.

Knockings and scrapings sounded from dead astern. That was our blind spot, full of auxiliary driving-tubes, and it wasn't possible to see from inside what was going on. McNulty barked an order. Two engineers and a navigator beat it up to that end. There was no way of determining the capabilities of these things outside, but if they were busily detaching our interchangeable tubes, well, we'd be fastened to that spot forever.

"Time we made up our minds," suggested Jay Score.

"Meaning what?" McNulty inquired.

"Whether we go outside and meet them or blast off and leave them."

"Yes, yes, I know." McNulty was bothered and a little testy. "But we still don't know whether they're friendly or hostile. I can't assume that they are hostile and I daren't assume that they're not. We've got to be cautious. The Terrestrial authorities won't stand for any rough handling of natives without adequate reason." He sniffed disgustedly. "And that means if they *are* hostile we must run away or else sit here until they make our reasons adequate."

"I propose," offered Kli Yang, brightly, "that we open the starboard lock and whistle them a little tune. When one of them comes up we'll jerk him inside and let him look us over. If he displays understandable fondness for us we will kiss him. If he does not we'll eject him, in pieces."

Pr-r-r-ang! The loud clang came from the stern, echoed

and re-echoed all over the vessel. McNulty winced as he visualised one of his precious tubes springing from its patent socket. He opened his mouth to say something, shut it as a bellow of rage came from the engine-room. The next instant a terrific *crump* burst in the rear and the whole ship shot twenty yards forward in a belly-slide.

Helping the sprawling skipper to his feet, Jay Score said, "Looks like Chief Andrews has settled the question. Nobody's going to fool around with his pipes!"

An angry muttering continued to trickle out of the engine-room, a steady, determined rumble like that of a small volcano held in check. McNulty knew better than to try to tackle the outraged chief in his present bellicose mood.

Looking out the nearest port just as its light shot through once more, McNulty spotted a retreating mechanism almost caught by the stabbing beam. Frowning, he spoke to Jay Score rather than to the rest of us.

"We have a choice of two moves. Either we must blast off or stop them meddling with the boat. The first may mean losing the missing lifeboat for keeps. By the looks of things, the second will mean trouble aplenty." His roving gaze found Steve Gregory. "Steve, go and have one more try at raising that lifeboat. If you can't get it we'll radio instructions in the hope that they can receive them, after which we'll open a lock."

"Right, skipper." Steve departed, one brow still more or less on his forehead. He returned within five minutes. "Not a squeak."

"Have your guns ready, men. Move one of those lights into the starboard lock and aim it on the door-gap." He stopped as the *Marathon* gave a sudden lurch, moving through an arc of ten degrees, then sluggishly rolling back onto an even keel. "And mount a pom-pom beside the light."

His listeners scattered at top speed, leaving him with Jay Score and the two engineers who were shifting the searchlight.

"Whew!" breathed McNulty. "I don't care to think of

the power that can roll our tonnage the way it's just been rolled."

Clink-clink-clunk! The noise rang gong-like through the *Marathon's* hull and sounded loudly in the armoury where I was busy doling out lethal persuaders. Came a second lurch, more violent this time. The arc was at least fifteen degrees, but again the ship reacted by swinging upright.

Running out with an armload of belts for the pom-pom, I found Jay waiting by the inner door of the lock. The ship settled with a shudder. Jay didn't say anything, just stood there with his rubber-soled feet braced firmly on the steel checkerplates of the floor, his huge form erect, his glowing orbs watching the gradually turning disc of the outer door.

With everything ready, the weighty door wound inward along its worm, came to the end, drew free like a great metal plug. The control arm rolled the heavy mass aside and simultaneously the searchlight filled the gap with an eye-searing glare.

Many scufflings, clankings and scrapings sounded in the dimness beyond but for a long time nothing appeared in the opening. Probably they thought the new gap was nothing but another observation-port. Hushed with expectancy, we stood and waited, but still nothing showed itself.

Greatly daring, a Flettner computator named Drake stepped into the column of light, walked slowly along the treadless stepping-strip at the bottom of the circular door-gap, stood on the outer rim and looked down. The next instant he let out a startled cry and was snatched from sight.

A big, broad-shouldered, bandy-legged engineer had followed behind Drake, and with apelike speed reached out a thick, hairy arm to grab the disappearing man's harness straps. He missed, for a moment stood defeated on the brink before he in his turn gave a gruff bellow and was whisked into darkness. By now Brennand had got to the middle of the hole but stopped in his tracks when McNulty gave a warning shout.

Brennand wasn't taken. He contributed to the general yelp as something outside tried to snatch him out of the tunnel, yelped louder when a snaking Martian tentacle wound round his waist and lugged him back. It must have been an awful pull judging by the way Kli Yang's many great suckers flattened for anchorage on the floor.

With grim calmness, McNulty asked, "What was it, Brennand?"

Before the other could reply there came a tremendous banging and clanking immediately outside. A huge square-ended and shining shape struggled into the airlock opening. It faced the searchlight, being fully revealed in the glare. I had a good view of its boxlike front with a coiled copper antenna sticking out the top like a caricature of a curl, and with a pair of big lenses staring at the light with cobralike lack of emotion.

Without waiting for McNulty, the gunner at the pompom decided this was no time to write to headquarters about the matter. He let fly. The din was terrific as the weapon's eight barrels pounded like pistons and a stream of midget shells poured through the door-gap. The invading creature appeared to dissolve before our very eyes, bits of rended metal, splinters of glassy substance and empty shell-cases flying in all directions.

The invader no sooner had gone than another was there, peering into the inferno without a blink. Same square end, same copper antenna, same cold, expressionless orbs. That, too, flew to pieces. Another and another. The gunner was wild with excitement and busily cursing one of his left-side feeders for being slow at the loading-rack.

A brief silence followed the wrecking of the fourth alien, a silence broken only by the rattle of fresh ammunition-belts being draped around the pom-pom.

"Well, the authorities at home can't complain about this," decided Captain McNulty. "Not after I've had two men taken, not to mention the lifeboat." He seemed to derive much comfort from the thought that his conscience was clear.

Somebody pounded down the passage and into the lock, said to him, "Number three light just showed Drake and Minshull. They've been carried away."

"They aren't in the danger zone, then?" chipped in Jay Score. "Good!" His eyes on the door-gap, he posed

42

with a casual air while his right hand juggled one of those eggs known as a pocket A-bomb. Up and down, up and down, with a horrible nonchalance that made me want to scream and jump on my dental plates.

"For Pete's sake, quit doing *that!*" protested someone who felt the same way I did.

Jay glanced around to see who was stroking a rabbit's foot. His eyes were cold, cold. Then he thumbed the projecting stud, tossed the egg through the gap into outer darkness. Everyone immediately grovelled, tried to push his own face through the floor and dig deep into bare earth, McNulty included.

There came a flash of supernal brilliance followed by an awful roar that rolled the ship sidewise onto its opposite atmospheric fin. After that, several slow heaves as of an earthquake.

A mutilated length of metal tentacle flew in from the dark, going, *whoo-whoo* with sheer speed, and cracked against the wall. Something faintly resembling the big end of a nautical telescope ricochetted off the pom-pom shield, zipped over the crouching skipper's fat, uplifted beam, skinned one of my earlobes, scored a long, yellowish mark along the steel floor.

If we expected more and lengthier silence outside, we were mistaken. The reverberations of the explosion had only just died away when a noise of violently torn metal came from the *Marathon's* stern, clanking feet and clattering claws hammered inward. Way back past the engine-room somebody yelled bloody murder, choked, gurgled.

Alien monstrosities surged full pelt into the airlock as perforce we turned to face this assault from a new direction. The pom-pom gunner stuck to his post and—ignoring what was taking place behind his back—concentrated on shooting a clear way through the outer door-gap. But via the mutilated stern, the passages and catwalks, a metallic zoo poured upon us.

The next two minutes fled like two seconds. I saw a wheeled globe whirl into the room, followed by a nightmarish assortment of metal things, some with jointed legs and pincer-armed front limbs, some with tentacles, some with a grotesque assortment of outlandish tools.

A grabbing pincer glowed red-hot and seized-up at the hinge when a well-aimed needle-ray found its weak spot. But its coffin-shaped owner pressed on as if nothing had happened, its projecting lenses staring glassily. In the hazy throw-back from the searchlight I saw Wilson burn away a lens-collar and deprive it of an eye before it snatched him up and held him.

The pom-pom suddenly ceased its rabid yammering and fell onto its side. Something cold, hard and slippery coiled around my waist, lifted me bodily. I went over backward through the lock, borne high in the unrelenting grip of my captor. I saw a many-tooled object grab the skipper's struggling form and bear him from the fray in like manner.

My last view of the mêlée showed a wildly gesticulating metal globe apparently floating toward the ceiling. It was fighting at the end of a thick, sucker-surfaced rope that would not let it go. McNulty and his captor blotted out the rest, but I guessed that one of the Martians had stuck himself to the roof and was blandly fishing in the mob below.

At a fast jog-trot the thing holding me set off toward the dimly glowing horizon. Dawn was breaking, with sunup due in twenty minutes. The landscape cleared rapidly.

My bearer was holding me down upon the flat of his long, level back, a taut cable around my chest, another around my waist, a many-jointed arm holding my legs. My feet were free to waggle around and my right hand still gripped a heavy needle-ray, but I was held far too tightly to bring the weapon to bear where it could do any good.

A dozen yards behind, McNulty was being lugged along like a bag of meal. His carrier differed from mine, being bigger, heavier, with eight multiple-jointed legs, no tentacles, but a dozen arms of various lengths. Four of its arms were holding down the writhing skipper, the two front ones were extended in imitation of a praying mantis, the rest were folded at its sides. I noticed that every now and again the contraption's grotesque copper curl would flip out straight, quiver questioningly, then abruptly coil like a watch-spring.

We passed other machines. A large group of them hung around the *Marathon's* damaged stern, big ones, small ones, squat ones, tall ones. Among them loomed the monstrous automaton with the steam-shovel hand. It squatted imperturbably at the end of a deep channel scooped from the ground below the ship's stern tubes. Half a dozen machines were extracting the bottom tubes. The top ones already were out and lying on the ground like so many drawn teeth.

"Well," I thought, with a deal of bitterness, "so much for Herr Flettner and his genius. If that bigbrain had never been born I'd now be sitting pretty aboard the good old *Upsydaisy*."

The thing on which I was having an unwanted ride began to increase pace, building up to a lumbering gallop. I couldn't twist round far enough to make an examination of it. The grips upon me were firm, unyielding and painfully tight. I could hear the metal pads of its feet clattering with noisy energy on the semi-metallic ground; but all I could glimpse was a rocking leg-socket that oozed a strong-smelling mineral oil.

Behind, McNulty's mount also accelerated. The light grew stronger. I raised my head as much as I could, saw a veritable procession of burdened machines stretching back to the ship. It was not possible to identify the various victims from my point of disadvantage.

A thrumming in the hazy sky drew my attention. Night had not sufficiently withdrawn her darkening hand and I failed to see the rocketships though I could follow their progress as steadily they blasted from north to south.

After more than an hour, my captor stopped and put me down. We must have covered somewhere about thirty miles. I ached all over. By this time the sun was up and we were at the verge of a wide, smooth road surfaced with dull, lead-coloured metal. A coffin-shaped object about seven feet long—the fantastic horse I had ridden upon the flat of my back—surveyed me through its horribly unemotional lenses.

Still retaining its grip, it shoved me through the doorway of a waiting vehicle. This was a big, boxlike affair mounted on double tractors and had the inevitable copper antenna protuding from its top. I had just time to note a

45

dozen similar tumbrils lined up behind when I was thrust into darkness.

The skipper followed me half a minute later. Then Brennand, Wilson, a computator and two engineers. The skipper was wheezing deep down in his chest. The engineers were using an amazing mixture of Terrestrial, Venusian and Martian oaths.

The door banged and locked itself, apparently of its own accord. The machine jerked as if prodded by an invisible finger, trundled forward at fair speed. It stank of oil. Somebody sniffed and sniffed and did some vituperative muttering in the gloom. I think it was Brennand.

Finding his automatic lighter, the skipper flicked it and we had a look around. Our moving prison proved to be a steel cell nine feet long by six wide. There wasn't so much as an ventilator. The oil-smell grew to an unbearable pungency.

Still sniffing and muttering, the offended Brennand raised his needle-ray and started to cut a hole in the roof, so I got mine going and speeded up the glowing circle. Metal flowed easily. The severed plate dropped out in a couple of minutes. If our carrier had any sentience, it remained unaware of its own mutilation for it kept going straight ahead without pause or falter.

The sky didn't show through the roof. No vision of fleecy clouds greeted us, no welcome flood of light poured in. Above the gap in the steel lay a thick coating of dark green stuff impervious to our needle-rays. We concentrated all we had upon it, without avail.

A try at the door and the walls brought no better result; green stuff again. The floor turned out to be the weak spot. As the machine roared onward, we cut a hole in the floor, light immediately sprang through it, we found ourselves staring down at a swiftly spinning shaft and a section of running road.

With his gun pointed downward, Brennand said, "Mother, see what I can do!" and cut the shaft.

The machine lost pace, stopped. We braced ourselves for an almighty crash that did not come. One by one the following machines swerved around us and kept going. Brennand and I continued to study the hole in the floor

46

while the others kept an anticipatory watch upon the door. McNulty and his computator had lost their weapons in the affray, but one of the engineers had retained his while the other engineer clung to a four-foot spanner with which—it was rumoured—he frequently slept.

We had no way of telling whether our dogbox had a driver or whether it functioned of its own volition or under some form of remote control, but if a driver or anyone else opened that door, we were all set to make a determined break. Nothing happened. We waited five tense minutes during which I wondered which of our crew were imprisoned in the other overtaking machines and to what sort of grim fate they were being rushed.

Finally we enlarged the gap in the floor and had almost made it big enough for our purpose when something huge and heavy churned along the road, hit our machine a gentle bump. Came a loud, metallic click and the next instant we moved forward, slowly, then faster. A breakdown dingus had come on the job.

The portion of road visible through the hole soon streamed past at a rate that put an end to any thought of escape via that route. To drop through would be foolhardy in the extreme; if we weren't chewed up by the speeding tractors we'd certainly be minced by anything that might be running close behind.

"This," remarked McNulty, "is most annoying."

"Annoying?" echoed Brennand, eyeing him peculiarly. He kneeled, put his face to the hole and enjoyed a few breaths of uncontaminated air. One of the engineers snickered.

"I have lost a seven hundred dollars owl-eye camera," announced young Wilson, with some ire. His eyes tried to stab the skipper to death. "That's a lot more than annoying! I'll take it out of their metal hides first chance I get!"

"Here's your blamed camera," announced Brennand. He got to his feet, extracted it from his pocket, handed it over, a thing little bigger than a cigarette pack. "You dropped it as you were lugged out of the ship. I caught it a moment before I was slung after you."

"Thanks—you're a pal!" Wilson fondled it with loving fingers. "I've been worrying about it." He stared straight at me, repeated, "Yes, I've been worrying about it."

47

One of the engineers glanced at the section of road flicking past the hole. The broken shaft, of course, was not rotating.

"We're being towed. If I were sure that nothing is following close upon us—" He let it hang a minute, then finished, "Hey, sit on my legs while I get my head through and have a look."

"No, you don't," snapped McNulty. "We're moving much too fast to risk a drop. We stay together and face events together."

So we sat on the floor wistfully watching the circle of light, our backs to the cold, hard walls. Somebody dug out an airtight can of cigarettes, opened it, handed it around. We smoked in glum silence.

Eventually our vehicle stopped and a multitude of grindings and clankings sounded all around. The entire machine shuddered as an unseeable enormity lumbered by at one side, shaking the ground with its tonnage. On the other side, something purred like a dynamo as it approached our door. We stood facing the door, alert, wide-eyed, those who had ray guns holding them ready.

With surprising swiftness the door clicked and swung wide. A big, multi-jointed arm reached through the opening, felt blindly around. The way it did it reminded me of a pet-store dealer groping in a box for white mice. I was still gaping at that shiny limb, my needle lined on its backmost joint, when one of the engineers ducked under it and leaped out whooping defiance.

The fantastic searcher was just about to fasten upon the skipper when the back joint seized as the ray hit dead on and the whole arm lost its flexibility. It withdrew, stiff and awkward, as the second engineer charged forth in the wake of the first. This one was the guy with the four-foot spanner. The silliest thoughts occur to one at the most inappropriate times; I remembered as I followed the computator and McNulty close upon this fellow's heels that at no time had I seen him put down that spanner or let go of it for a moment.

Outside the battle was short and sharp. We found ourselves faced by forty machines of eight distinct types. Half a dozen of them were no bigger than dogs and did nothing but canter around observing everything that happened. The biggest was a monstrosity twice the size of a Pullman coach and had one great, telescopic arm terminating in a huge, black disc.

Five yards from the door, struggling in the grasp of a many-armed coffin, the engineer who'd got out first was striving to burn away the contraption's near-side lens. The one with the spanner had tangled with a wheeled globe and battered ineffectually at the universal joints from which its writhing tentacles sprouted. He was cursing with great vigour and admirable fluency.

On the left a tall, idiotic gadget faintly resembling a drunken surrealist's notion of a sober giraffe, was running away with McNulty. It had four arms that tightly embraced the luckless skipper, four legs that moved in ungainly swings, and a greatly elongated neck from the top of which shone a single lens. Still full of life, the skipper was putting up a futile struggle.

With its front limbs thrown out in mock affection a glassily staring coffin thumped forward to clasp me to its bosom. It moved with the dull, heavy *dum-dum-dum* you hear in Africa when an enraged rhinoceros is making for you. A belly-fluttering sound. It was so near that I sensed its characteristic stink of warm machine oil.

I stepped backward beyond what I thought would be the limit of its full reach and promptly it slid another twenty inches of joint from its metal casing. That trick almost cost me my unwary head. I tripped and went down in the nick of time, felt its bear-trap hand swipe across my top hairs.

There was something ghastly about the silence of this battle. Our opponents made no sound in any way vocal. Except for our own oaths and grunts nothing could be heard but the smooth purring of hidden works, the swish of metal tentacles, the clank of jointed arms, the thud of massive metal feet.

My opponent snatched downward as I dropped, but I rolled as never I'd rolled before, dodged both its grab and its pounding legs. My needle-ray spiked at its flat underside and did no good whatsoever. Twisting clear, I sprang to my feet, glanced rightward, saw the computator's body lying in one place and his brains in another. I felt sick.

As I swung to watch the coffin, the Pullman thing—which had taken no part up to then—aimed its disc at me and bathed me from head to feet in a powerful beam of pale-green light. Theoretically, as I discovered later on, that beam should have jammed my radio animation and made me stiffer than that stuff they call Rigor Mortis. But since I had non-mechanical animation of my very own the device remained nothing more than a pale-green light.

The globes were by far the speediest of all this crazy assortment of super-gadgets and it was a globe that got me in the end. My coffin-shaped opponent lumbered clumsily around to have another go at me, another coffin galloped toward me from the opposite side, and as I tried to divide my attention between both, a globe nipped in from behind and laid me out.

At one moment my ray was pouring its thin blade into the body of the nearest oncomer while over its sights I had a view of McNulty and the giraffe retreating far behind my attacker's back, then—*thunk!*—the universe exploded in my head, I let go my weapon and collapsed.

McNulty called the roll. Tattered and weary, but his plump little form still in one piece, he stood with his shoulders squared back and looked us over. Jay Score posed beside him, big and solid as ever, his stallite chest sticking out through the shreds of his uniform, but his eyes glittering with the old, everlasting fires.

"Ambrose."

"Here, sir."

"Armstrong."

"Here, sir."

"Bailey."

No reply. The skipper glanced up, frowning.

"Bailey. Does anyone know what has happened to Chief Steward Bailey?"

Somebody said, "Haven't seen him since just before the fight on the ship, sir." Nobody added to this information.

"Humph!" McNulty's frown deepened. He marked his list and continued. I was puzzled as I looked over our mauled but still tough gang. Something missing, something missing. But either the skipper hadn't sensed it or else he was ignoring it, for he proceeded methodically with his task. "Barker, Bannister, Blaine, Brennand . . ." Again his eyes lifted as there came no response.

"Brennand was in our dogbox," I reminded. "I don't know what happened to him."

"You can't say definitely that he's dead?"

"No, sir."

"Brennand never came out of that machine," offered a voice. It was the gentleman with the spanner. He stood beside the eyebrow-waggling Steve Gregory, and his face looked like a half-eaten orange, but still he was attached to his hunk of iron. Maybe the machines had let him keep it because they'd mistaken it for part of his arm. He said, "I was the last to go under in that free-for-all. Brennand wasn't taking part. Neither was Wilson."

McNulty registered a touch of woe; Jay Score showed a little interest. The skipper made two marks on his list and carried on. It wasn't until he reached the letter K that I discovered the missing factor nagging my subconscious.

"Kli Dreen, Kli Morg, Kli . . . where's Kli Dreen?"

We started around, the whole bunch of us. Not a Martian among those present. Not one. Kli Yang, Sug Farn and the rest—nine in all—were missing. Neither could anyone remember seeing them after the struggle in the *Marathon*. The last man out of the vessel had been Murdoch, a government expert, and he swore that when he got snatched the Martians were still aboard and still fighting. Leastways, none of them had been tossed into his vehicle, the last of the line.

We could think up no satisfactory explanation of Martian escape from durance vile, nor hazard a guess at their present state. Perhaps their enormous strength had prevailed against the metal monstrosities, though that didn't seem likely. My private notion, which I kept strictly to myself, was that they'd managed to get the foe crazy about chess and right now both sides were waiting breathlessly for someone to jump a bishop two squares. The Martians were fully capable of a stunt as lopsided as that.

Marking all the Red Planet names, McNulty continued to the bottom of his list, omitting Sixth Engineer Zeigler in the same way that he'd omitted Chief Andrews, and

51

for the same reason. Those two were known to be dead. They'd succumbed to that first onslaught through the stern.

Summing up, McNulty found seven dead, five missing, not counting the Martians. The missing consisted of Haines and his two men in the lifeboat, also Brennand and Wilson. This was a serious loss to our small company and our only comfort lay in the thought that the missing ones nevertheless might be alive.

I took stock of our prison while the skipper mooned sadly at the roll. We were in a metal barn, a great, bare place a hundred feet long by sixty wide by forty high. Its walls were smooth, drab-coloured, windowless. The deeply curved roof, equally drab, was devoid of any opening, but from its apex hung three large spheres of translucent plastic that glowed with orange light. Closely as I examined the walls I could not find upon their dead flat surface a single line or solitary flaw suggestive of a butt weld or any other kind of joint.

"Well, men——" began McNulty.

He got no further. Thinly, eerily, a long-drawn scream trickled through the thin cracks around the building's only door. It was a high-pitched sound thrust up to the very peak of agony and it had many reverberations as if escaping through a long, metal corridor. Above all, it was a human voice—or the voice of what was left of something human.

The men milled around, their foreheads glossy with perspiration. Murdoch looked sheet-white. Sam Hignett's black fingers opened and closed as they itched to go to the aid of the sufferer. The engineer with the spanner had rolled up his sleeves and revealed a tattooed nautch dancer on the muscle of his lower left arm. The dancer shimmied as he changed and tightened his grip on the spanner. His face still looked terrible, but his eyes were hard.

Slowly, Jay Score expressed the general feeling by saying, "If we had the handling of one of these automatons we'd pull it to pieces to see what makes its cuckoo call the hours." He stared at nobody in particular. "In that respect, they may resemble us, much as I hate to admit it. Any man who doesn't fancy being picked to bits to

52

satisfy alien curiosity had better take care that they never get him out of here alive!"

Again the terrible scream. It broke off abruptly the moment it reached its top note and ensuing silence seemed as horrible as the noise. I could imagine them now, clicking and whirring as they moved around, looking in vain for the fleshly apparatus that had produced the sound—their metal claws smeared with red as they pawed at what had been a living thing.

"Are there any acrobats in the house?" inquired Jay, suddenly.

Walking to the wall, he faced it, planted big hands against it, braced his feet on the floor. Armstrong, a powerful six-footer, scrambled up him, stood on his shoulders. That much was easy but the rest was not.

By dint of much clumsy struggling we got Petersen's feet firmly set on Armstrong's shoulders. Petersen's head was now fifteen or sixteen feet above floor level. No matter how we tried we could not lengthen the human ladder. Jay Score stood like a rock but the smooth wall offered no grip permitting his double burden to steady themselves as another man tried to top them. We had to give it up.

No doubt about it, Jay could have supported the seven men needed to reach the roof, assuming that Armstrong could bear his six. I could see no point in trying for the roof, anyway. All the same, this futile effort served to occupy our hands and minds for a short while.

Blaine tried his needle-ray on the wall with the obvious idea of cutting a series of foot-holds, but this stuff proved much different from that with which the vehicles were built. It heated up quite normally, turning primrose colour at maximum temperature, but flatly refused to melt or be cut.

This attempt with the ray gave the skipper the notion of making an inventory of available weapons. Between the lot of us there were seven ray guns, one ancient vest-pocket automatic pistol the owner of which claimed that it had been used by his father in the Final War, one four-foot spanner, two tear-gas pencils.

Events had shown the ray guns to be a fat lot of use against our armour-plated enemies. The rest of the stuff was mere lumber. But the inventory served to reveal one interesting angle of the foe's psychology in that anyone who'd clung grimly to his weapon had been permitted to keep it. This suggested that they didn't know weapons when they saw them!

We'd just finished inspecting this inadequate armament when the door shot open with suddenness that caught us napping and two lobsterlike things were thrust into our prison. The door shut with a vicious clash, giving us not the slightest glimpse of what lay beyond it. Skidding helplessly across a corner of the metal floor, the lobsters brought up against the wall in a manner that laid them flat. For a moment they reposed there while we stared at them fascinatedly and they gaped back at us. Recovering, they came to their legs. It could now be seen that their heads more resembled those of insects than of lobsters, for they had multiple-lensed eyes and butterfly antennae.

Getting over their surprise, these creatures talked to us, not vocally, but with quasi-telepathic speech that seemed to pop up inside our brains. Their weird mouths never opened, their palps did not move, but so efficient was their projection of thought-forms that it was difficult to believe they weren't addressing us in our own language. It was a feat very much like the iguana's.

One of them—I couldn't decide which one—said, "You are strangers from some other place. You are soft-bodied things, quite unlike the hard-shelled things of our solar system. Can you understand us?"

"Yes," replied McNulty, bugging his eyes at them. "We understand you."

"Sound waves!" The strange pair stared at each other in mutual dumbfoundment, their delicate antennae quivering. I could almost hear the ejaculation-mark at the end of their comment. "They communicate by means of modulated sound waves!" For some reason best known to themselves, this verged on the incredible. They gazed at us as though we outraged a basic law of nature, then, "You are difficult to talk with. You do not assist with your minds. We have to push in our thoughts and pull out yours."

54

"I'm sorry," apologized McNulty. He gulped, composed himself. "Mental communication is not our speciality."

"It is of no consequence. We are managing." Each of them made identically the same vague gesture with the same claw. "Despite our differences in shape and form, it is apparent that we are brothers in misfortune."

"At the moment," agreed McNulty, refusing to see anything permanent about this status. He was now beginning to regard himself as something of a universal contact-man. "Have you any idea of what they intend to do with us?"

"They'll dissect you."

"Dissect us? Cut us up?"

"Yes."

McNulty scowled and asked, "Why?"

"They dissect all the individualistic. They've been doing it for years, centuries, trying to discover the cause of personal independence. They are intelligent machines, but their intelligence is completely communal." The lobster, or whatever it was, mused and went on, "Upon our own world of Varga there are tiny aquatics of similar type in that they're nothing remarkable as individuals but display high intelligence when functioning in organized groups. They share a racial mind."

"Like certain termites," suggested the skipper.

"Yes, like termites," confirmed whichever of the two was doing the mental talking—or was it both? I couldn't see how he—or they—could agree about termites of which they knew nothing until I remembered that what was in the skipper's mind had been impressed on their minds, too. "For many, many circumsolar revolutions they have been trying to conquer the neighbouring water-world of Varga, which is our home planet. Our people have resisted with some success but occasionally some of us are captured, brought here and dissected."

"They *are* only machines, though?"

"They are machines of a large number of functional types, all kinds of warriors, all kinds of workers, even experts and specialists. But they are machines." He stopped, shocked us to the marrow by suddenly pointing an accusative claw at the silently watching Jay Score. "Just

55

as *he* is a machine! He is made of metal and his mind remains closed to us! We do not like him!"

"Jay's a lot more than a mere machine," declared McNulty in open indignation. "He's got something no stinking gadget ever had. I can't explain what is it, but . . . well . . . he's a person."

A low murmur showed that he had expressed the irrational but nonetheless convinced opinion of his crew.

"What I've got is no more than the general complaint," suggested Jay, unsmiling. "I've got independence. That makes me a candidate for the butchers along with the rest." He sighed, added, "I suppose I'll go the way of all flesh."

Grinning at this pessimistic sally, McNulty said to the abashed lobster-things, "If you are sensitive to the thoughts of our kind you might be able to tell us whether you can detect any human emanations from elsewhere. A few of my men are missing and I'd like to know whether they're still alive."

The pair of strange creatures from Varga went quiet while their antennae trembled as if delicately searching a portion of the ether beyond our range and comprehension. Something rumbled noisily along the corridor and passed our door without stopping, but they took no notice of this diversion.

After a while one of them—or both—said, "Our range is short, exceedingly short. We can tell you that a mind like yours has just gone away, gone forever. It petered out even as we were conversing. There are no other minds of your type within receptive distance."

"Oh," said McNulty, disappointed.

They pointed claws toward the roof and went on, "But up there there are other minds far stranger than yours, far different from ours. They are unique. We would not have thought them possible. Unbelievable as it may be, they can concentrate upon two subjects at one and the same time."

"Eh?" said McNulty, scratching his head. He could make nothing of this information.

"Two subjects at once! Most remarkable! They are high up in the air but descending toward the roof. One of them is thinking of an array of little gods on a square

56

composed of coloured squares and is also thinking of . . . *you!*"

"What?" McNulty shouted.

I saw Steve Gregory's scalp swallow his eyebrows as he followed the skipper's example and stared wildly upward. We all looked pop-eyed at the roof. Next instant came a tremendous thump that shook the place from end to end and a huge dent appeared in the curve of the roof. Something hammered violently on the metal plates, other things created an uproar in the corridors beyond the door. The combined noises were awful; I felt like a bug in a boiler with half a dozen riveters at work on the seams.

Our unofficial spanner-bearer was one guy with observation and initiative. He'd noticed that the door opened inward. With his hefty four-foot instrument still in one fist, he crammed his other hand into a back pocket, felt around, proved himself tough enough to think nothing of sitting on two short, thick screwdrivers and a small lump of metal shaped like an axe-head. These items he walloped into the base of the door, performing the task with some difficulty, but finally managing to wedge the thing good and tight. He'd barely finished when the row in the corridor increased and a great weight made the door groan.

It looked as though our time had come, delayed a few precious minutes by the fastened door. Those clanking enormities outside were thirsty for samples to slice apart. Our much-prized individualism was to be our downfall. On this basis it struck me that the spanner-holder and Sam Hignett might be chosen for first carving if the carvers had any preferences, because they'd be curious about why the former possessed a half-metal, double-length arm and why the latter had a black skin in contrast with everyone else's white. I also wondered what would be their reaction when they got the measure of Jay Score.

The door shook to a terrific blow, did not turn on its hinges but did begin to bulge in the middle. Brilliant light streamed through the gap between its bent top edge and the wall. Caterpillar treads rattled past outside while the mechanism thrusting at the door maintained its powerful pressure.

"Don't shoot until you see the green of their teeth,"

grinned the door-wedger. He spat on the floor, leaned on his spanner like a waiting knight leaning on his mace. The pose made his tattooed nautch dancer look incongruous.

Came a loud tearing sound from the roof as a great section of it was pulled away bodily. Sunlight poured over our upturned faces. A large, leathery, bulbous body with many huge, sucker-surfaced arms tumbled over the ragged rim, clung with three of its snaking limbs and hung grotesquely in mid-air. It was Sug Farn.

Adding three more tentacles to those maintaining his overhead hold, he extended the remaining four downward. His full spread was thirty-two feet, now reduced by five or six feet of sucker-hold upon the roof. His tentacle tips dangled and curled enticingly a good fourteen feet from the floor. The door made an alarming bend inward while Sug Farn hung there and we looked up at him with various degrees of hope. The lobster creatures surveyed him aghast.

Then suddenly he came down another ten feet, grabbed four of the crew, swung them up to the hole in the roof. They went like mahouts lifted in elephants' trunks. Eyeing the hole, I could see that Sug Farn no longer had any direct hold of his own, his upper tentacles being closely entwined with the equally ropey limbs of another Martian anchored out of view on the roof-top. Sug Farn raised the four to within a few feet of the hole whereupon other tentacles writhed through from above, took them from him. Then four more and four more.

What with trying to keep my attention divided between this circus act and the dangerously creaking door, I hadn't taken overmuch notice of the Vargans, but now I discovered they were having a bitter argument with McNulty.

"No," declared the skipper, firmly. "We do not give in. We do not face the inevitable. We do not die with aplomb, as you put it." He sniffed his disgust. "We had a tribe on Earth that looked at things your way. They celebrated their miseries with nonchalant belly-slitting. It never got them anywhere."

"But escape simply isn't done," the Vargans persisted, as though talking about a war atrocity. "It is dastardly. It is contrary to convention. It is outrageous defiance of the accepted rules of war. Even a child knows that a prisoner

58

must maintain honour by uncomplainingly accepting his fate."

"Bunk!" snorted McNulty. "Balderdash! We're not on parole. We've made no promises and don't intend to make any." He watched another four sail upward to freedom.

"It is wrong, utterly wrong. It is disgraceful. A captive is lost forever. Why, our own people would kill us from sheer shame were we to go away. Have you no conscience?"

"Your rules are idiotic," McNulty said. "We aren't bound by them. We don't subscribe to them. No matter what you say, it's perfectly legitimate for us to—"

"Listen!" interjected Jay Score. His glowing eyes shifted from the expostulating skipper to the partially wrecked door which now threatened to give way at any moment. "This is no time to debate different codes of ethics!"

"Sure, Jay, but these hard-shelled dunderheads—*ouch!*" His surprised expression was comical as the imperturbable Sug Farn fished for him, got him and lugged him clean out of the argument.

The door gave way at last, bursting with a sound that tore the ears. Not counting the defeatist Vargans, there were seven of us remaining on the floor when the door fell in and a thing like a fifty ton tank rumbled headlong into the busted jail.

A clicking, whirring mass of coffins, globes and other nightmarish contraptions crowded hard behind it. The leading invader was so big it filled the large doorway with only a couple of inches to spare on either side. Fascinatedly, too fearful to move, I watched its great caterpillar treads streaming downward over the front cog-drives as it lumbered toward me, an alien juggernaut.

His black features curiously alight, Sam Hignett yelled at Sug Farn, "Me last!"

Our Negro surgeon might have got his self-sacrificing wish, but he counted without the tentacled individual dangling overhead. A speedy globe got through the doorway, beat the juggernaut along the floor and grabbed at Sam. It was about two seconds too late. Silently, without comment or visible excitement, Sug Farn released

59

three of his clinging arms from the roof, garnered all seven of us and with a mighty effort heaved us beyond reach.

As I slowly soared to the hole I could feel a subtle trembling in the limb lifting me while Sug Farn strained his utmost to raise the big burden. Another limb reached down, coiled around me, took some of the weight. Up through the hole I caught a glimpse of another Martian figure crawling along the underside of the dented roof toward the top of the nearer wall, then I was in the sunlight and on my feet.

Sitting in its handy roof-dent like a mud-hen on its nest was the pinnace. There the powerful little vessel rested, its tubes ready for action, its smooth, streamlined shape a thing of delight. No vision could have done more to boost the spirits of weary men.

Metal buildings towered all around us, most of them with roofs higher than the one on which we were standing. Square or oblong in plan, without windows, or decorations of any sort, all were severely and depressingly utilitarian. No smoke or steam arose from any point within view, but puffs of coloured vapour came from several invisible sources.

Many of the buildings bore great latticework radio masts; a few had complicated aerial arrays resembling directional antennae. The entire place was a metal metropolis.

Down below, wide, straight, evenly-spaced streets were filled with scurrying machines of at least a hundred types. Most of them looked like nothing we'd formerly seen; one in particular, a long, semi-flexible contraption, reminded me of a monster centipede. It had a triple row of revolving cutters projecting from its front and evidently functioned as some sort of tube borer or subterranean excavator.

A small proportion of coffins and globes were visible among the crowd, with a couple of giraffes and several of those inquisitive, seemingly useless gadgets that had got under our feet during the earlier affray. Observing this medley of alien forms, I developed the notion that the globes and coffins were different kinds of warriors, the giraffes were civil police and that the nosey little machines were reporters or war correspondents who kept constant watch and transmitted continual reports either to some co-ordinating centre or maybe to the community as a whole. But I didn't feel too sure about the giraffes.

While two-thirds of the rescued crew clambered into the pinnace, giving it a full load, I stood with Jay Score at the ragged edge of the roof-hole and looked in on our recent prison. It was an amazing sight. The pair of lobster-things had gone, presumably to their anticipated fate. Immediately beneath us, squatting like an enormous iron toad in the middle of the floor, was the fifty tonner that had burst in through the door.

Around it glassy-eyed globes whirled hither and thither, occasionally waving tentacles at us in what could have been fury—if an automaton is capable of fury. Several coffins had folded their jointed rear legs, sat and stared up at us in fantastic imitation of a pack of baulked hounds, their forward lenses having gained enough tilt to bear on the roof and reveal their escaped prey. Despite their total lack of facial animation I could almost see their jaws open and tongues hanging out. Most of the moving machines made a continual clicking and clanking. Their pungent oil smelled to high heaven.

Thirty feet above this mob, Sug Farn and Kli Yang had stuck themselves securely to the tops of opposite walls and now fished for the enemy. Sug Farn snaked out a tentacle that looked as though it could have anchored a battleship, spread the end suckers on the flat, smooth back of a squatting coffin which—to judge from its posture—was patiently waiting for us to drop like over-ripe grapes. Sug Farn lifted the coffin which immediately clanked with alarm and waved its jointed legs. An alert globe whirled to its rescue.

Kli Yang at once chipped in and took the globe with all the blank-faced nonchalance of a chameleon tongue-swatting a fat fly. The coffin soared twenty-five feet, the suckers let go, it dropped on the back of the fifty tonner, crashed thence to the floor with a rattle of busted internal works and lay motionless. The globe, which was lighter, went up fighting madly in the sucker-grasp of Kli Yang, then was flung on top of another globe. The flung one went dead. The struck one suffered some sort of injury to its steering circuits and proceeded to race round and round in a tight circle.

Looking longingly at the biggest monstrosity which continued to sit unmoving beneath us with all the indifference of a dumped flivver, Kli Yang remarked, "This is how we won the fight in the ship. We sat on the ceilings where they couldn't get at us. We picked them up, dropped them and left the rest to nature. They can't climb. Neither could they get into the *Marathon* a machine big enough to reach us."

With one saucer eye on me and Jay, he rolled the other downward for another look at the foe. This independent swivelling of Martian eyes always did give me the creeps and always will. To Sug Farn, he added, as if it were a logical afterthought on the same subject, "Kli Morg ought to have sacrificed his bishop."

"Yes, I have just reached that solution," agreed Sug Farn, using a globe to crack the pate of a giraffe. "Morg tends to err on the side of economy in his games. That makes him somewhat slow to see that the loss of a bishop now is well worth the gain of two rooks ten moves later." He sighed, said, "Watch this!" made a swift snatch at a gesticulating object that seemed to be a mass of weird tools, got it by a big knobbed projection on its front, hurled it against the base of Kli Yang's wall.

Whoom! Heat bathed my legs as the pinnace blew free and drummed into the sky. That left eleven of us on the roof plus the double-minded Martians amusing themselves by converting our prison into a junk-yard. Turning, I saw the pinnace zooming northward on a stream of thunder and fire.

"They'll be back for us shortly—if we're still here." Jay Score's brilliant optics studies the Martians and the metal horde below. "Kli is wrong in suggesting that they have no climbers. How did they erect these buildings?"

"None of those can climb," I argued uneasily, pointing to the crowd down there.

"No—but I bet they have some kind of building machines stowed away, some kind of mechanical steeplejack. Ten to one they will haul them out as soon as they get over the confusion we've caused by defying their rules of war." He indicated surrounding streets in which no great excitement was yet evident. "It is taking a long time to sink in. I doubt whether a prisoner has ever broken free within living memory, if they have memories. Temporarily they are stumped by a situation they can hardly comprehend."

"Yes, we certainly are dealing with a totally different kind of mentality," I agreed. "It looks as if they're too conditioned to meet the abnormal and cope with it promptly."

I didn't mention it because Jay was too much of a definite personality, but I felt that he had some advantage over the rest of us in being able to look at things from the viewpoint of our mechanical opponents.

Kli Yang crawled up through the hole, followed by Sug Farn. The latter stared around, settled himself in the dent made by the pinnace, wrapped himself up in his own tentacles and went to sleep. From him came high, soft and long-drawn whistles.

"Slumbering!" complained Kli Yang. "He cannot do anything without grabbing himself a sleep on the strength of it." Keeping one disgusted eye fixed on the snoring Martian, he swivelled the other toward Steve Gregory. What with his off-centre eyes and Steve's jiggling eyebrows, I began to wonder what hidden talents I might possess. "I suppose," said Kli Yang, gloomily, "it didn't occur to anyone in the pinnace to leave a chess-board behind?"

"No, it didn't," Steve admitted, secretly thankful for the omission.

"It wouldn't," grumbled Kli Yang. Edging away from us, he dug out a tiny bottle of *hooloo* scent, sniffed at it pointedly. I suppose the twelve pounds pressure was beginning to get him down. I never did believe those indecent Martian descriptions of the human odour.

"How did you know which building we were in?" Jay Score inquired.

"We came drumming over," Kli Yang told him, "with poor hope of finding you in this jumble of edifices. We circled around several times and were much surprised that the mob of things in the streets took not the slightest notice of us. Eventually we saw that line of parked vehicles with Brennand and Wilson standing on top of one signalling frantically. So we picked them up and landed on this, the nearest roof. Our drop was slightly clumsy because the pinnace is hard to handle with controls made for human limbs."

"Brennand and Wilson are safe then?" I put in.

"Yes. Kli Dreen yanked them into the boat. They said they'd got out of their vehicle through the hole in its floor instead of the door, after which they were completely ignored. They were amazed by the way in which they'd been left alone and they couldn't understand it."

Glancing at me, Jay said, "See—escapees! The abnormal factor! Nobody knew what to do about them. They were in blatant denial of local ethics, a problem that required time to solve solely because new and previously unknown."

He strolled to the edge of the roof, his crepe-rubber soles carrying his weight silently on the smooth surface. Another roof adjoined ours, but on a lower level. He stared down at it, his eyes aglow.

"Those screams came from somewhere under there. Come on, let's see whether we can tear up a corner and have a look at what's beneath."

He dropped four feet onto the lower roof, followed by Armstrong, me and the others. Together we heaved and strained at a lapping metal corner. It gave way, coming up with unexpected ease. That metal was darned peculiar stuff, fairly hard, impervious to heat, yet bendable along the line of a hidden grain. No wonder the Martians had been able to rip a hole in the roof.

Peering through the gap, we found a long, narrow room that might have been either a laboratory or an operating theatre. Apparatus of all kinds littered it, including radiant lamps, sterilising chests, trays of peculiar instruments, wheeled tables, and an assortment of junk we couldn't recognise.

Half a dozen highly polished and superbly finished machines were busy in this room, their shiny, unemotional lenses intent on their tasks. They had dexterous digits. What they were doing gave me the willies.

Two lobster-things were spread all over the room, part of one on a near table, two heads on another, a mass of innards on a third. Whether they had been the same pair with which we had talked or whether they were two others, it was impossible to tell. The machines were fooling around with the bits, putting sections under odd-looking microscopes, sticking pieces into various kinds of apparatus.

The lobsters had nothing recognisable as blood but their mutilated parts exuded an oily, colourless juice. All the same, there were significant daubs of crimson on one of the unoccupied tables, spots of crimson on the floor, spatters of crimson on a couple of the mechanical vivi-sectionists. In a wire basket, carelessly tossed aside, lay a pair of human hands. The left one, white and flaccid, still bore a gold signet ring. It had belonged to Haines!

Armstrong cursed violently and said, "What wouldn't I give to be able to blow this place to shreds."

"There's nothing we can do—yet," commented Jay Score, not visibly moved. "We're too late to save any-one." He eyed the next roof which lay on the same level and about twenty-five feet away. Like the outpiece on which we were standing, it projected from a bigger and higher building surmounted by a tall radio mast. Twin antennae ran from this mast to another on a matching edifice a hundred yards off. "I think I can jump that gap." Jay murmured.

"Now take it easy," advised Armstrong, looking over the edge at the big drop under that twenty-five foot chasm. "Wait until the pinnace comes back. If you try a leap of this description and fail to make it by a couple of inches, you'll go down fast and far. You'll be converted into a thousand souvenirs scattered over the street."

Returning to the hole in our roof, Jay glanced down through it. "They are still waiting," he reported, "but they won't wait for ever. They're likely to go into action before long." He came back, the tattered rags of his uniform flapping around his great stallite legs. "So I'd better have a little action on my own account."

Before any of us could make a move to prevent him, he'd measured his pace and started. There was no stop-ping him once he was on his way: his solid and powerful three-hundred or more pounds made too much mass for mere human muscles to oppose. Kli Yang, perhaps, might have done it, but he didn't try.

With a superswift and well-timed run, Jay shot off the rim of our roof, arced over the intervening street, landed with a good yard to spare. A second and easier jump carried him to a higher level. Reaching the lattice-mast, he went up it like a monkey and tore away its antenna. Then he returned; the same spectacular leap performed with the same margin.

"Some day," suggested Kli Yang, comfortingly, "you will get yourself electrocuted—if you don't first break your neck." He gestured to the street. "It may be coincidence or it may not, but some of those machines have quit moving."

It was true. Amid the hurly-burly below a number of automatons had become lifeless as statues. They were all of the same kind. Other types were unaffected and jostled around as of yore. Coffins, globes, wormlike things and large, lumbering mock-bulldozers went about their business as though nothing had occurred, but the few specimens of this one particular type—an egg-bodied, spindle-legged device—posed like ones petrified in their tracks.

"I'd say they have radio-animation," ventured Jay. "Each kind has its own waveband and its own station from which it draws power." He pointed to other masts sticking up all over the city. "If we could put those out of action, I think we'd stiffen the lot into temporary immobility."

"Why temporary?" I asked. "To deprive them of power would be rather permanent, wouldn't it?"

"Not necessarily. There's such a large variety of machines designed for every imaginable function that ten to one they've also got an independently-powered radio repair squad which would come to life the moment everyone else went dead."

Someone interjected, "If their radio mechanics look anything like an ambling lighthouse, there's one on his way here already." He jerked an indicative thumb northward.

We looked that way. The object coming down the north road was fantastic in the extreme. It consisted of a long metal platform running on huge wheels ten to twelve

66

feet in diameter. From the centre of the platform rose a gradually tapering tubular body terminating in a many-lensed, many-armed top piece more than sixty feet above ground-level. The thing seemed taller than a fire-tower, dominating the street and some of the buildings.

"Clap hands—here comes Charlie!" said the gentleman who owned the ancient pistol. He gripped the out-of-date weapon with much determination. Compared with the on-coming colossus, the pistol was absurd. One might as well hope to bring down a rogue elephant with spit-balls.

"An automatic erector, I think." Jay watched it coolly, calmly. "Probably it has been summoned to pick us off."

The little gang of humans seemed unconcerned about the matter. Maybe they were trying to conceal feelings like those bubbling in my own insides. As the tremendous menace rumbled slowly and inevitably nearer, my stomach shrank to a small, hard ball.

Down in the street the mechanical horde still went to and fro, while beneath the hole in the roof waited another hungry pack. Jay might be able to get away by means of his mighty leaps from rooftop to rooftop, but the rest of us could do nothing but wait like steers in a slaughter-house.

Then a dot appeared in the sky and a high-pitched whine told us that the pinnace was coming back. A swift little bullet, it dived toward us at full pelt. As nearly as I could judge it was likely to reach our precarious perch slightly ahead of the threatening tower-contraption, but I doubted whether it could land, open its airlock, take us aboard and blow free before trouble started. Our pulses working overtime, we watched the swift onrush of the pinnace, the weighty forward trundle of the super-sized foe, and anxiously compared the progress of both.

Just as I'd decided that half of us might make it at the expense of the other half, those in the pinnace saw the advancing tower. The vessel made no attempt to land. Describing a tight half-turn that rocked it laterally, it shot over us with a screaming rush of air, cut across the head of the tower now a mere fifty yards away. A midget atomic bomb must have dropped, though I didn't see it go down.

"Drop!" rasped Jay Score, urgently.

We flopped on our faces. Something whooped sky-high, our building swayed, a rare assortment of hardware fountained up from the street. For a few seconds there was an eerie silence broken only by the composite clankings of survivors of the metal population and the receding howl of the pinnace. Then came a great crash as the towerlike mechanism fell headlong. The building shuddered again.

I clambered to my feet. The tower reposed full length in the street, its platform wrecked, its long, tubular body twisted and distorted, its lensed and many-armed head battered out of recognition and devoid of animation. The fallen giant had put an end to a dozen smaller machines with its collapse.

Sug Farn, violently awakened, chirruped, "What's all the row about? Are they at it again?" He stretched his tentacles, yawned.

"Get out of that dent," ordered Kli Yang, looking at him with disfavour. "Make room for the pinnance."

Without haste and with poor grace, Sug Farn moved over to a corner of the roof where we formed a tiny, hopeful group. Zooming round in a shallow sweep, the pinnace came in, settled down, landed. Under its weight, the dent in the roof became slightly deeper, more pronounced. But for immense supports beneath the roof, and the expertness of the vessel's landing, the little ship might have burst clean through the plates and thrown the lot of us into the enemy's power.

Thankfully we piled into the boat. The skipper wasn't aboard and neither was Brennand. Second Navigator Quirk held the controls and had a crew of five Terrestrials and one Martian, the minimum for a vessel of this size. The Martian was Kli Dreen. He didn't say a word to his snaky-armed fellows as they squirmed through the lock, merely stared at them and sniffed.

"I will bet twelve interplanetary dollars," Kli Yang told him, acidly, "that your underworked brain never thought of bringing our low-pressure helmets so that we could find relief from this infernal smell."

"Hear him!" appealed Kli Dreen, swivelling one eye

68

toward me. "He explores the universe and then complains about a little pressure." The eye rolled back to Kli Yang as he added triumphantly, "Kli Morg would have won if he hadn't insisted on saving his bishop."

"Ha-ha!" Kli Yang laughed with artificial violence. He tried to wink knowingly at Sug Farn, and failed. The Martians frequently tried to imitate the Terrestrial habit of significantly closing one eye; they kept on trying despite the dismal fact that it can't be done without eyelids. "A week late in seeing the solution, as usual!"

I found young Wilson standing by the forward observation port, near Pilot Quirk. The camera lay ready in his hands and he fairly drooled. Two more cameras sat in holding-straps on the wall, one of them an instrument with a lense the size of a saucer.

"Oh, sarge," he yammered at me. "Shots, shots, shots—dozens of them." His face was magenta with professional glory. "And I got that tower-thing the moment we bopped it. Watch me get these two as well."

Peering over his shoulder I had a look through the port. Sure enough two more of the lofty erections were coming down the street, swaying like drunken sailors as they progressed. Back of me I could hear our airlock door being wound home.

Wilson's camera went click-click. The pinnace stirred, swept away from the roof, boosted speed under Quirk's expert hands. No Martian could handle a boat with quite the same touch as a well-trained Terrestrial.

I went in search of Jay Score, found him prone by the little bomb hatch in the belly. He was holding a banger and released it just as I got there. Putting my face to the nearest port, I saw the building adjoining our former prison bulge at the walls and throw its roof at the clouds. The inside must have been a shambles.

"So much for their operating-theatre," growled Jay. His eyes were like coals. "That one took *them* apart for a change!"

I could sympathise with his feelings but, darn it, a robot isn't supposed to experience so human an emotion as a thirst for revenge. Still, nobody cared to show surprise at his rare moments of unrobotic sentiment. By all the laws he wasn't supposed to have any more feelings than a dummy—but the fact remained that he did have them, in a cold, phlegmatic sort of way.

"McNulty won't like that," I pointed out. "He'll say that despite our losses the Terrestrial authorities will call it unnecessary destruction. He'll let his conscience nag him all the way home."

"Of course," agreed Jay, with suspicious alacrity. "I did not think of that. What a pity!" His voice hadn't altered its inflection in the slightest degree while his face, of course, remained completely without expression. His thoughts were as easy to read as those of a stone joss.

He went forward to see Quirk. Soon afterwards we made a series of swoops as steadily we drummed northward. Each time the boat ducked down there came a resounding twang from outside, so I had another go at the port, found we were busting a few antennae on our route. I didn't need extra-sensory perception to know that Jay had a hand in that performance, whether McNulty approved or not.

Quickly the great metropolis rolled away beneath us, its roads dotted with hurrying machines plus a good number that were stalled, unmoving. Back in the distance I could just make out the pair of towers which by now had reached our recent sanctuary. One track minds; they had been ordered to do a job and were still trying to obey a full minute after we'd gone.

That city covered twenty square miles and all of it metal. I've never seen so much metal in one place, nor think I'll ever do so again.

Out here in the suburbs the egg-bodied machines remained in sweet repose along with three other kinds, and I could see various individuals hors-de-combat on the wide arterial roads running north and south.

Whang! went another antenna, then we soared to twenty thousand feet. On the southern horizon a second city now revealed faint outlines of high buildings and tall masts.

Like a beautiful golden spindle the *Marathon* lay on the black and crimson surface. Most of the crew were busy around her stern. Diving to her starboard side, the pinnace landed and we poured out. It wasn't until that moment I remembered that my belly had been empty for hours.

We heard the other part of the story over a quick and more than welcome meal. It appeared that the Martians had coped with all attacks until the globes and coffins withdrew. These had posted themselves at a short distance from the ship and waited for nobody knew what; perhaps for the Martians to come out and be flattened in the open or, more probably, for the arrival of some other kind of machine better able to deal with them.

The Martians had seized this opportunity to blow free in the pinnace and had seen their beseigers swarm into the abandoned vessel the moment they left. But except for wrecked specimens lying around, the hostile horde had gone by the time we returned.

"You know," pondered Jay Score, "it looks rather as if mere motion is their definition of sentient life. It moves, therefore it lives. The *Marathon* has no animation of its own, so they considered it as being no menace in itself. They were after the crew. When the crew were all gone, they bothered no more about the ship." His eyes examined us speculatively. "Nobody's thought of trying it, but it's possible that if you're cornered and stand perfectly motionless, they might leave you alone. Yes, they might at that! But if you move, they're after you forthwith!"

"I wouldn't care to try that no-motion stunt," said a voice, dryly. "Give me my feet every time. And, Mister, let 'em be fast feet!"

"Wonder if they'll attack again, before we've completed repairs," I ventured.

"There's no knowing. In my opinion, they've a most curious mentality, if you can call it that," Jay went on. "They accept the familiar, are instinctively and immediately hostile towards the unfamiliar. The vessel was assaulted solely because it was an unknown interloper. By this time it's probably recorded in their communal mind as a known wreck of no particular consequence. It won't be until some passing machine reports unrecorded activity here that the communal mind may connect it with our escape, ponder what should be done about it, then order that it be done." He glanced through a port

71

toward dusty hills half shrouding the setting sun. "We'd better move fast."

Beating it outside we lent a hand at the tough job of resocketing the stern tubes. It was one heck of a task, using an inadequate derrick and manhandling the great pipes into position. Meanwhile, the Martians repaired the torn stern, their welding machines flashing brilliant blue. Engineers went over the combustion-chambers, checking efficiency. Three more made good the damage done in the nearby airlock, mostly by the pom-pom.

Quirk took the pinnace over to the far road while we were engaged in these tasks. The skipper didn't want him to risk it, but he hung high in the clouds until the road was temporarily free of traffic, shot down and found the missing lifeboat. Three of his crew brought it back together with the bodies of Haines' two companions.

As far as we could tell from the available evidence, the lifeboat had landed openly and in friendly fashion with Haines unaware that a waiting Pullman-thing had blanked out his radio channel. Haines had been captured. The other two had gone down fighting and been left—motionless. We buried them in the evening along with Chief Andrews and the others.

Long after dark the blue flashes of Martian welders cut through the night and steady hammerings sounded in various parts of the vessel. We were doing plenty to advertise ourselves and no doubt about it, but risks have to be taken.

All this time McNulty alternated between ill-concealed gloominess and high spirits. I reckon the former was due to anticipation of another attack before we had finished. The latter might have been because we were making ready to blow free, or perhaps because we'd gained a cargo of astonishing specimens in the shape of three wrecked globes and two smashed coffins. Our attackers had taken away all the remaining junk or, to put it another way, had removed the rest of their wounded from the battlefield.

At two o'clock the following afternoon the tedious task was finished with a few loud hurrahs and a few more sulphurous versions of the same. We blasted off. Down in the cargo-hold the government experts gloated over our load. Soaring miles above the scene of recent troubles, we reached the second city in the south, touched ground near its outskirts.

"Here we should be a new factor," remarked Jay Score. "Let's see how they take it."

I timed it by my watch. The attack came in exactly thirty-seven minutes.

The local technique was different. First of all the reporters came along, carefully inspected us with many skitterings around then hastened back to the city. Next, a dozen Pullman-sized gadgets waddled up, aimed their discs at us and bathed the entire vessel in their rays. Steve Gregory immediately shot out of his room complaining that his radio had gone haywire. He illustrated the trouble by violently oscillating his brows.

Outside, more forces joined the futile disc-manipulators. Things with enormous hands, things with a multitude of built-in tools, all made for our stern. The inevitable array of coffins and globes scouted warily around.

Two giraffes turned up and unknowingly posed for young Wilson. By now the skipper decided that we had waited long enough and had better not give the opposition any time to meddle with the stern-pipes. With a terrific *whoosh!* that misted the landscape we shot skyward, leaving them flustered and defeated.

Twenty minutes afterward we plunked down within easy reach of a wide but little used road and waited for something to come along on its ownsome. The first arrival proved to be a galloping coffin with eight steadily thumping legs, four folded arms, two tentacles in front, its idiotic copper curl unwound and sticking straight up like a solitary hair. Half a dozen of us barred its way, our ray guns aimed more as a gesture than anything else. They weren't much of a threat to these metal things, as we knew only too well.

It was all Jay's idea to which McNulty had consented with much reluctance. The skipper agreed to the ambush only on condition that we arranged it near enough to be covered by one of the *Marathon's* pom-poms. I could see the fast-firing weapon's eight barrels peering from the nearest lock as the coffin slowed its pace, then stopped.

Six more of the crew got into the road behind our victim, another four covered the side opposite the *Marathon*. The coffin looked us over, its lenses hard, shiny and without expression, its copper antenna quivering questionably. I had a strange notion that somehow its horde already knew about its predicament and were summoning the riot squad. I also knew that if it chose to charge blindly ahead, we could do nothing to stop it. The metal mass could go through our ranks like a knife through cheese.

For a few breathless moments the alien entity stared at us and we stared back. Then it lumbered around preparatory to beating a retreat, found itself cut off, turned to face its original direction. We looked at each other until the silence and the tension became unbearable. Still the thing did not stir a limb.

"As I thought, just a metal hick," said Jay, blandly ignoring the fact that he wasn't skin and bone himself. Boldly he walked to within three or four feet of the coffin, gestured toward the *Marathon,* beckoned and walked away.

A beckon is unmistakable in any language, on any world. I certainly didn't expect that grotesque thing to obey the gesture. But, so help me, it did!

With his broad back turned to the coffin, Jay marched toward the ship and the coffin came to life and followed him with the slow, meek gait of a dejected horse. That was the only time I've seen the spanner-holder gape and let go his tool.

Meeting a pop-eyed McNulty at the lock, Jay said, "See, it has crazy ethics. It believes it is my prisoner and therefore must face its fate." Leading it inside, he conducted it to the hold, parked it in a corner where it stood obediently, without overt move. "Chances are it will become lifeless the moment we get beyond the sphere of power-radiation from which it draws its vim. We had better let Steve play with it: maybe he'll be able to restore its animation with some sort of portable power-pack."

"Humph!" said McNulty, staring owlishly at the coffin. He turned to Blaine. "Tell Steve to come down here."

The surrender of a potentially tough specimen occupied our minds as we fastened the locks and prepared to take off for keeps. Apparently the things would give battle in squads but not as individuals. One could not look into that coffin's mind—if it had a mind other than its share of the communal consciousness—but we wondered whether, like the lobsters, it was now fated to meet death at the hands of its fellows if ever it returned.

Their way of looking at things was crazy and craziest of all was their intolerance of initiative such as we possessed. Or was it really so lunatic by comparison with the ethics of humans? Maybe it all depends on what is meant by 'human'. I'm no profound scholar, no expert in history, but I seemed to recall a long-gone war far, far back in the dark ages, when the Japanese refused to admit they had any men missing and callously declared them dead.

But it wasn't long before we learned that corporate mentalities have advantages as well as disadvantages. We blew free from the black and crimson ground, shot skyward for the last time on this cockeyed world, burst through the clouds and promptly encountered four long, black rocketships. They were vessels such as we'd seen previously and they squirted along in perfect line.

There was no question of the leader spotting us and issuing orders to the others. They saw us simultaneously, reacted simultaneously, moving in remarkable and impressive unison. It made me think of a major scientific mystery, namely, that of how a flock of birds often alter course, change formation, wheel, form and turn like creatures governed by one mutually shared mind. These ships duplicated the bird trick. They switched course together, cut into our path in echelon formation, bathed us in the same useless rays that had failed to affect us before but again got Steve Gregory mad. I had never witnessed such perfect teamwork.

It did them no good, did us no harm. Had their rays functioned as they were expected to do we'd soon have been a smoking heap on the ground beneath. Diving through the aura, we zoomed on toward free space. They followed, changing to line-abreast with mathematical precision, nosing upward at identical angles as though one man were handling all four by remote control. Together they blew their auxiliaries, spurted along our trail, narrowed the margin between us.

"Pretty fast," commented Jay. "About as fast as we are when running in normal drive. I'd certainly like to have a look at their engines and pilots."

"I've no desire to see them," grunted McNulty. "I've had enough of them for one trip." He bawled into the engine-room phone, the *Marathon* heeled over, plunged sickeningly, shot upward again. Glassware broke in the galley and somebody offered loud and vulgar opinions about ships that dipped and captains who made them dip. The pursuing quartet heeled, plunged and rose behind us in unison.

Greenish rays reached out for us once more, flickered without avail, then four streaks of fire flashed by on one side. They even missed by precisely the same margin!

"That's enough to be going on with," declared McNulty, not inclined to tempt fate. He gave the *Marathon* an S-turn, said curtly, "Straps!"

We'd barely time to jump into harness before he threw her in Flettner drive. I couldn't see them because you can't use the observation-ports while prostrate, but the quartet behind must have shrunk to vague dots in the space of one heartbeat. At uncatchable velocity we went out of that solar system, skimming by the water-world of Varga so fast that nobody saw it. That lump of cosmic plasma and its amphibious inhabitants would have to wait until some other trip.

All the way home the Martians kept to the starboard lock enjoying its three pounds pressure and their everlasting chess. Jay spent much of his time down in the cargo-hold along with Steve—presumably nursing the dumb coffin—but the Martians did chivvy him into having seventeen games of which he won three. They gloated and published the figures all over the ship.

Wislon remained in his cabin brooding. I wasn't foolish enough to ask any questions or try to comfort him. The clumsy warriors of Mechanistria had converted his first few plates to splinters while cavorting around the ship, but his subsequent shots were large in number and beauti-

76

ful in execution. He was determined to worry them safely home.

Two cruisers met us outside Terrestrial atmosphere, escorted us down. The old, familiar browns, blues and greens of Earth made the loveliest sight I've seen, though the Martians still preferred dirty pink and said so. They were arguing with some heat over a lost pawn when we landed with the whole world watching and listening via the international network.

McNulty made the speech expected of him. "We have had a somewhat difficult time . . . unquestioning hostility that is much to be deplored . . . this uncomfortable episode." And so on and so on.

Flettner was duly exhibited in front of us, blushed like a kid at McNulty's frequent references to the efficiency of the ship in which, for once, he didn't resort to understatement.

Back of the crowd of greeters I saw old Knud Johannsen, the robot master, struggling to get through and anxiously looking for Jay. Sometimes I wonder whether I have precognition for—although I didn't know what was coming—the sight of that white-haired old wizard wanting to meet his last and greatest creation made me think of a fond father seeking his son.

The rah-rahs ended and we began to unload. Cans of coppery water, flasks of compressed alien air, hundreds of samples of earths and metals were lugged out. We produced the busted automatons and the government experts rushed away with them as if they were transferring the jewels of Asia. Wilson departed even faster, bearing his plates and several cans of film.

Old Knud extracted himself from the onlooking mob, said to me, "Hello, sergeant—where's Jay?" He had no hat and his silvery locks gleamed in the sun.

Jay emerged from the lock at that moment. His shining eyes found the white-haired figure waiting for him. You know, robots can't make wisecracks, they just can't—and Jay had never made one in his existence, leastways, not a recognisable one. But this time he made one of the best I've ever heard and it brought a slight lump into my sentimental gullet.

Taking Knud's thin, veined hand in his huge metal paw,

77

he said, "Hello—Dad!" I couldn't see Knud's fond face, but I heard Jay add, "I've brought you an interesting souvenir."

He gestured toward the lock from which came a loud clanking and a whiff of pungent oil. The captive coffin emerged, its copper curl coiled up and attached by a wire to a black box on its back. Steve Gregory walked behind it, his eyebrows lopsided with gratification.

Arm in arm, Jay and Knud strolled away, the alien automaton following close behind, Steve trailing in the rear. I lost sight of them when two special-delivery toughies started to haul up the gangway an enormous vase of horrible shape and revolting colours.

Reaching the top, one of them produced a paper, surveyed it with distaste and informed, "This super-gobboon is for a Snake-arms named Kli Morg."

"I'll go tell him." As a precautionary afterthought, I said, "Meanwhile, you'd better return it to ground-level—the skipper won't have it on board."

They broke it on the way down.

SYMBIOTICA

They had commissioned the *Marathon* to look over a likely planet floating near Rigel and what some of us would have liked to learn was how our Terrestrial astronomers could select worthwhile subjects at such an enormous distance.

Last trip they'd found us a juicy job when they'd sent us to that mechanical world and its watery neighbour near Boötes. The *Marathon,* a newly designed Flettner boat, was something super and had no counterpart in our neck of the cosmos. So our solution of the mystery was that the astronomers had got hold of some instrument equally revolutionary.

Anyway, we had covered the outward trip as per instructions and had come near enough to see that once again the astronomers had justified their claim to expertness when they'd said that here was a planet likely to hold life.

Over to starboard, Rigel blazed like a distant furnace about thirty degrees above the plane which was horizontal at that moment. By that I mean the horizontal plane always is the ship's horizontal plane to which the entire cosmos had to relate itself whether it likes it or not. But this planet's primary wasn't the far-off Rigel: its own sun —much nearer—looked a fraction smaller and rather yellower than Old Sol.

Two more planets lay farther out and we'd seen another one swinging round the opposite side of the sun. That made four in all, but three were as sterile as a Venusian guppy's mind and only this, the innermost one, seemed interesting.

We swooped upon it how first. The way that world swelled in the observation-ports did things to my insides.

One trip on the casually meandering *Upsydaisy* had given me my space-legs and made me accustomed to living in suspense over umpteen million miles of nothingness, but I reckoned it was going to take me another century or two to become hardened to the mad bull take-offs and landings of these Flettner craft.

Young Wilson in his harness followed his pious custom of praying for the safety of his photographic plates. From his expression of spiritual agony you'd have thought he was married to the darned things. We landed, *kerumph!* The boat did a hectic belly-slide.

"I wouldn't grieve," I told Wilson. "Those emulsified window-panes never fry you a chicken or shove a strawberry shortcake under your drooling mouth."

"No," he admitted. "They don't." Struggling out of his harness, he gave me the sour eye and growled, "How'd you like me to spit in the needlers?"

"I'd break your neck," I promised.

"See?" he said, pointedly, and forthwith beat it to find out whether his stuff had survived intact.

Sticking my face to the nearest port, I had a look through its thick disc and studied what I could see of the new world. It was green. You'd never have believed any place could be so thoroughly and absolutely green. The sun, which had appeared a primrose colour out in space, now looked an extremely pale green. It poured down a flood of yellow-green light.

The *Marathon* lay in a glade that cut through a mighty forest. The area immediately around us was lush with green grasses, herbs, shrubs, and bugs. And the forest itself was a near-solid mass of tremendous growths that ranged in colour from a very light silver-green to a dark, glossy green that verged upon black.

Brennand came and stood beside me. His face promptly became a spotty and bilious green as the eerie light hit it. He looked like one of the undead.

"Well, here we are again." Turning away from the port, he grinned at me, swiftly wiped the grin off his face and replaced it with a look of alarm. "Hey, don't you be sick over me!"

"It's the light," I pointed out. "Take a look at yourself.

You resemble a portion of undigested haggis floating in the scuppers of a Moon-tripper."

"Thanks," he said.

"Don't mention it."

For a while we remained there looking out the port and waiting for the general summons to the conference which usually preceded the first venture out of the ship. I was counting on maintaining my lucky streak by being picked from the hat. Brennand likewise itched to stamp his feet on real soil. But the summons did not come.

In the end, Brennand griped, "The skipper is slow— what's holding him?"

"No idea."

I had another look at his leprous face. It was awful. Judging by his expression he wasn't fanatically in love with my features either.

I said, "You know how cautious McNulty is. Guess that spree on Mechanistria has persuaded him to count a hundred before issuing an order."

"Yes," agreed Brennand. "I'll go forward and find out what's cooking."

He mooched along the passage. I couldn't go with him because at this stage it was my duty to be ready at the armoury. You never could tell when they'd come for the stuff therein, and they had a habit of coming on the run.

Brennand had only just disappeared around the end corner when sure enough the exploring party barged in shouting for equipment. Six of them. Molders, an engineer; Jepson, a navigating officer; Sam Hignett, our Negro surgeon; young Wilson, and two Martians, Kli Dreen and Kli Morg.

"Hah, lucky again?" I growled at Sam, tossing him his needle ray and sundry oddments.

"Yes, sergeant." His very white teeth glistened in his dark face as he smiled with satisfaction. "The skipper says nobody is to go out afoot until first we've scouted around in number four lifeboat."

Kli Morg got his needler in a long, snaky tentacle, waved the dangerous thing around with bland disregard

81

for everyone's safety, and chirruped, "Give Dreen and me our helmets."

"Helmets?" I glanced from him to the Terrestrials. "You guys want spacesuits, too?"

"No," replied Jepson. "The stuff outside is up to fifteen pounds and so rich in oxygen you whizz around thinking you're merely ambling."

"Mud!" snapped Kli Morg. "Just like mud! Give us our helmets."

He got them. These Martians were so conditioned by the three pounds pressure of their native planet that anything thicker and heavier irritated their livers, assuming that they had livers. That's why they had the use of the starboard airlock in which pressure was kept down to suit their taste. They could endure weightier atmosphere for a limited time, but sooner or later they'd wax unsociable and behave as though burdened with the world's woes.

We Terrestrials helped them clamp down their head-and-shoulder pieces and exhaust the air to what they considered comfortable. If I'd lent a hand with this job once I'd done it fifty times and still it seemed as crazy as ever. It isn't right that people should feel happier for breathing in short whiffs.

Jay Score lumbered lithely into the armoury just as I'd got all the clients decorated like Christmas trees. He leaned his more than three hundred pounds on the tubular barrier which promptly groaned. He got off it quickly. His eyes shone brightly in a face as impassive as ever.

Shaking the barrier to see if it was wrecked, I said, "The trouble with you is that you don't know your own strength."

He ignored that, turned his attention to the others and told them, "The skipper orders you to be extra careful. We don't want any repetition of what happened to Haines and his crew. Don't fly below one thousand feet, don't risk a landing elsewhere. Keep the autocamera running, keep your eyes skinned and beat it back here the moment you discover anything worth reporting."

"All right, Jay." Molders swung a couple of spare ammo belts over an arm. "We'll watch our steps."

They traipsed out. Soon afterwards the lifeboat broke free with a squeaky parody of the *Marathon's* deep-throated, sonorous drumming. It curved sharply through the green light, soared over huge trees and diminished to a dot. Brennand returned, stood by the port and watched the boat vanish.

"McNulty is leery," he remarked.

"He has plenty of reasons. And he has all the explaining to do when we arrive home."

A smirk passed over his seasick complexion. "I took a walk to the noisy end and found that a couple of those stern-gang bums have beaten everyone to the mark. They didn't wait for orders. They're outside right now, playing duck-on-the-rock."

"Playing *what?*" I yelped.

"Duck-on-the-rock," he repeated, deriving malicious satisfaction from it.

I went to the tail-end, Brennand following with a wide grin. Sure enough, two of those dirty mechanics who service the tubes had pulled a fast one. They must have crawled out through the main driver, not yet cool. Standing ankle-deep in green growths, the pair were ribbing each other and slinging pebbles at a small rock poised on top of a boulder. To look at them you'd have thought this was a Sunday school picnic.

"Does the skipper know about this?"

"Don't be silly," advised Brennand. "Do you think he'd pick that pair of unshaven tramps for first out?"

One of the couple turned, noticed us staring at him through the port. He smiled toothily, shouted something impossible to hear through the thick walls, leaped nine feet into the air and smacked his chest with a grimy hand. He made it plain that the gravity was low, the oxygen-content high and he was feeling mutinously topnotch. Brennand's face suggested that he was sorely tempted to crawl through the tube and join the fun.

"McNulty will skin those hoodlums," I said, dutifully concealing my envy.

"Can't blame them. Our artificial gravity is still switched on, the ship is full of fog and we've come a long, long way. It'll be great to go outside. I could do some sand-castling myself if I had a bucket and spade."

"There isn't any sand."

Becoming tired of the rock, the escapees picked themselves a supply of round pebbles from among the growths, moved toward a big bush growing fifty yards from the *Marathon's* stern. The farther away they went, the greater the likelihood of them being spotted from the skipper's lair, but they didn't care a hoot. They knew McNulty couldn't do much more than lecture them and enter it in the log disguised as a severe reprimand.

This bush stood between twelve and fifteen feet high, had a very thick mass of bright green foliage at the top of a thin, willowy trunk. One of the pair approached it a couple of yards ahead of the other, flung a pebble at the bush, struck it fair and square in the middle of the foliage. What happened next was so swift that we had difficulty in following it.

The pebble crashed amid the leaves. The entire bush whipped over backwards as if its trunk were a steel spring. A trio of tiny creatures fell out at the limit of the arc, dropped from sight into herbage below. The bush whipped forward in a return swipe and then stood precisely as before, undisturbed except for a minute quivering in its topmost branches.

But the one who'd flung the stone now lay flat on his face. His companion, three or four paces behind, had stopped and was gaping like one petrified by the utterly unexpected.

"Hey?" squawked Brennand. "What happened there?"

Outside, the man who had fallen suddenly stirred, rolled over, sat up and started picking at himself. His companion got to him, helped him pick. Not a sound came into the ship, so we couldn't hear what they were talking about or the oaths they were certainly using.

The picking process finished, the smitten one came unsteadily erect. His balance was lousy and his fellow had to support him as they started back to the ship. Behind them the bush stood as innocent-looking as ever, its vague quivers having died away.

Halfway back to the *Marathon* the pebble-thrower teetered and went white, then licked his lips and keeled over. The other glanced anxiously toward the bush as if he wouldn't have been surprised to find it charging down upon them. Bending, he got the body in a shoulder-hitch, struggled with it toward the midway airlock. Jay Score met him before he'd heaved his load twenty steps. Striding powerfully and confidently through the carpet of green, Jay took the limp form from the other and carried it with ease. We raced toward the bow to find out what had happened.

Brushing past us, Jay bore his burden into our tiny surgery where Wally Simcox—Sam's sidekick—started working on the patient. The victim's buddy hung around outside the door and looked sick. He looked considerably more sick when Captain McNulty came along and stabbed him with an accusative stare before going inside.

After half a minute, the skipper shoved out a red, irate face and rapped, "Go tell Steve to recall that lifeboat at once—Sam is urgently needed."

Dashing to the radio-room, I passed on the message. Steve's eyebrows circumnavigated his face as he flicked a switch and cuddled a microphone to his chest. He got through to the boat, told them, listened to the reply.

"They're returning immediately."

Going back, I said to the uneasy duck-on-the-rock enthusiast, "What happened, Stupid?"

He flinched. "That bush made a target of him and filled his area with darts. Long, thin ones, like thorns. All over his head and neck and through his clothes. One made a pinhole through his ear. Luckily they missed his eyes."

"Yeah!" said Brennand.

"A bunch of them whisked past me on my left, fell twenty feet behind. They'd plenty of force; I heard them buzz like angry bees." He swallowed hard, shuffled his feet around. "It must have thrown a hundred or more."

McNulty came out then, his features somewhat fierce. Very slowly and deliberately he said to the escapee, "I'll deal with you later!" The look he sent with it would have scorched the pants off a space cop. We watched his portly form parade down the passage.

The victim registered bitterness, beat it to his post at the stern. Next minute the lifeboat made one complete circle overhead, descended with a thin zoom ending in a heavy swish. Its crew poured aboard the *Marathon* while derricks clattered and rattled as they swung the boat's twelve-ton bulk into the mother ship.

Sam remained in the surgery an hour, came out shaking his head. "He's gone. We could do nothing for him."

"You mean he's—dead?"

"Yes. Those darts are loaded with a powerful alkaline poison. It's virulent. We've no antidote for it. It clots the blood, like snake venom." He rubbed a weary hand over his crisp, curly hair. "I hate having to report this to the skipper."

We followed him forward. I stuck my eye to the peephole in the starboard airlock as we passed, had a look at what the Martians were doing. Kli Dreen and Kli Morg played chess with three others watching them. As usual, Sug Farn snored in one corner. It takes a Martian to be bored by adventure yet sweat with excitement over a slow-motion game like chess. They always did have an inverted sense of values.

Keeping one saucer eye on the board, Kli Dreen let the other glance idly at my face framed in the peephole. His two-way look gave me the creeps. I've heard that chameleons can swivel them independently, but no chameleon could take it to an extreme that tied your own optic nerves in knots. I chased after Brennand and Sam. There was a strong smell of trouble up at that end.

The skipper fairly rocketed on getting Sam's report. His voice resounded loudly through the partly open door.

"Hardly landed and already there's a casualty to be entered in the log . . . utter foolhardiness . . . more than a silly prank . . . blatant disregard of standing orders . . . sheer indiscipline." He paused while he took breath. "Nevertheless the responsibility is mine. Jay, summon the ship's company."

The general call blared as Jay pressed the stud. We barged in, the rest following soon after, the Martians arriving last. Eyeing us with an air of outraged authority, McNulty stutted to and fro, lectured us to some length.

We'd been specially chosen to crew the *Marathon* because we were believed to be cool, calculating, well-disciplined individuals who had come of age, got over our weaning, and long outgrown such infantile attractions as duck-on-the-rock.

"Not to mention chess," he added, his manner decidedly jaundiced.

Kli Dreen gave a violent start, looked around to see whether his tentacled fellows had heard this piece of incredible blasphemy. A couple indulged in underbreath chirrupings as they stirred up whatever they use for blood.

"Mind you," continued the skipper, subconsciously realising that he'd spat in somebody's holy water, "I'm no killjoy, but it is necessary to emphasise that there's a time and place for everything." The Martians rallied slightly. "And so," continued McNulty, "I want you always to——"

A 'phone shrilled, cutting him short. There were three 'phones on his desk. He gaped at them in the manner of one who has every reason to suspect the evidence of his ears. The ship's company stared at each other to see if anyone were missing. There shouldn't have been: a general call is answered by the entire company.

McNulty decided that to answer the 'phone might be the simplest way of solving the mystery. Grabbing an instrument, he gave it a hoarse and incredulous, "Yes?" One of the other 'phones whirred again, proving him a bad chooser. Slamming down the one he was holding, he took up another, repeated, "Yes?"

The 'phone made squeaky noises against his ear while his florid features underwent the most peculiar contortions. "Who?" "What?" he demanded. "What awoke you?" His eyes bugged. "Somebody knocking at the door?"

Planting the 'phone, he ruminated in faint amazement, then said to Jay Score, "That was Sug Farn. He complains that his siesta is being disturbed by a hammering on the turnscrew of the starboard airlock." Finding a chair, he flopped into it, breathed asthmatically. His popping eyes roamed around, discovered Steve Gregory. He snapped, "For heaven's sake, man control those eyebrows of yours."

Steve pushed one up, pulled one down, let his mouth dangle open and tried to look contrite. The result was imbecilic. Bending over the skipper, Jay Score talked to him in smooth undertones. McNulty nodded tiredly. Jay came erect, addressed us.

"All right, men, go back to your stations. The Martians

had better don their helmets. We'll install a pom-pom in that airlock and have the armed lifeboat crew standing by it. Then we'll open the lock."

That was sensible enough. You could see anyone approaching the ship in broad daylight but not once they'd come close up: the side ports didn't permit a sharp enough angle so that anyone standing right under the lock would be shielded by the vessel's bulge.

Nobody was tactless enough to mention it, but the skipper had erred in holding a revival meeting without maintaining watch. Unless the hammerers saw fit to move outward, away from the door on which they were thumping, we'd no means of getting a look at them except by opening the door. We weren't going to cook dinner and tidy the beds before discovering what was outside, not after that last nasty experience when hostile machines had started to disassemble the ship around us.

Well, the dozing Sug Farn got poked out of his corner and sent off for his head-and-shoulder unit. We erected the pom-pom with its centre barrel lined on the middle of the turnscrew. Something made half a dozen loud clunks on the outside of the door as we finished. It sounded to me like a volley of flung stones.

Slowly the door spun along its worm and drew aside. A bright shaft of green light showed through and with it came a stream of air that made me feel like a healthy hippopotamus. At the same time old Andrews' successor, Chief Engineer Douglas, switched off the artificial gravity and we all dropped to two-thirds normal weight.

We gazed at that green-lit opening with such anxious intentness that it became easy to imagine an animated metal coffin suddenly clambering through, its front lenses glistening in unemotional enmity. But there came no whirr of hidden machinery, no menacing clank of metal arms and legs, nothing except the sigh of this strangely invigorating wind through distant trees, the rustle of blown grasses and a queer, unidentifiable, faraway throbbing that may or may not have emanated from jungle drums.

So deep was the silence that Jepson's breathing came loud over my shoulder. The pom-pom gunner crouched in his seat, his keen eyes focused along the sights, his finger curled around the trigger, his right and left hand feeders ready with reserve belts. All three of the pom-pom crew were busy with wads of gum while they waited.

Then I heard a soft pad-pad of feet moving in the grass immediately below the lock.

We all knew that McNulty would throw a fit if anyone dared walk to the rim. He nursed annoyed memories of the last time somebody did just that and was snatched out. So like a gang of dummies we stayed put, waiting, waiting.

Presently there sounded a querulous gabble beneath the opening. Next moment a smooth rock the size of a melon flew through the gap, missed Jepson by a few inches, shattered against the back wall.

Skipper or no skipper, I became fed up, hefted my needler in my right hand, prowled half bent along the footwalk cut through the threads of the airlock worm. Reaching the rim which was about nine feet above ground level, I thrust out an inquiring face. Molders pressed close behind me. The muffled throbbing now sounded more clearly than ever, yet remained just as elusive.

Beneath me stood a small band of six beings startlingly human at first appearance. Same bodily contours, same limbs and digits, similar features. They differed from us mostly in that their skins were coarse and crinkly, a dull, drab-green in colour, and they had a peculiar organ like the head of a chrysanthemum protruding from their bare chests. Their eyes were jet black, sharp, and darted about with monkeylike alertness.

For all these differences, our superficial similarity was so surprising that I stood gaping at them while they stared back at me. Then one of them shrilled something in the singsong tones of an excited Chinese, swung his right arm, did his best to bash out the contents of my skull. Ducking, I heard and felt the missile swish across my top hairs. Molders also ducked it, involuntarily pushed against me. The thing crashed inside the lock, I heard somebody spit a lurid oath as I overbalanced and fell out.

Clinging grimly to the needle-ray, I flopped into soft greenery, rolled like mad, and bounced to my feet. At any instant I expected to see a shower of meteors as I was slugged. But the alien sextet weren't there. They were fifty yards away and moving fast, making for the shelter of the forest in long, agile leaps that would have shamed a hungry kangaroo. It would have been easy to bring two or three of them down, but McNulty could crucify me for it. Earth-laws are strict about the treatment of alien aborigines.

Molders came out of the lock, followed by Jepson, Wilson and Kli Yang. Wilson had his owl eye camera with a colour filter over its lens. He was wild with excitement.

"I got them from the fourth port. I made two shots as they scrammed."

"Humph!" Molders stared around. He was a big, burly, phlegmatic man who looked more like a Scandinavian brewer than a space-jerk. "Let's follow them to the edge of the jungle."

"That's an idea," agreed Jepson, heartily. He wouldn't have been hearty about it if he'd known what was coming to him. Stamping his feet on the springy turf, he sucked in a lungful of oxygen-rich air. "This is our chance for a legitimate walk."

We started off without delay, knowing it wouldn't be long before the skipper started howling for us to come back. There's no man so hard to convince that risks have to be taken and that casualties are the price of knowledge, nor any man who'd go so far to do so little when he got there.

Reaching the verge of the forest, the six green ones stopped and warily observed our approach. If they were quick to take it on the run when caught out in the open, they weren't so quick when in the shadow of the trees which, for some reason, gave them more confidence. Turning his back to us, one of them doubled himself and made faces at us from between his knees. It seemed senseless, without purpose or significance.

"What's that for?" growled Jepson, disliking the face that mopped and mowed at him from beneath a crinkled backside.

Wilson gave a snigger and informed, "I've seen it before. A gesture of derision———It must be of cosmic popularity."

"I could have scalded his seat if I'd been quick," said Jepson, aggrievedly. Then he put his foot in a hole and fell on his face.

The green ones set up a howl of glee, flung a volley of stones that dropped short of the target. We broke into a run, going along in great bounds. The low gravity wasn't spoiled by the thick blanket of air which, of course, pressed equally in all directions; our weight was considerably below Earth poundage so that we loped along several laps ahead of Olympic champions.

Five of the green ones promptly faced into the forest. The sixth shot like a squirrel up the trunk of the nearest tree. Their behaviour carried an irresistible suggestion that for some unknown reason they regarded the trees as refuges safe against all assaults.

We stopped about eighty yards from that particular tree. For all we knew it might have been waiting for us with a monster load of darts. Our minds thought moodily of what one comparatively small bush had done. Scattering in a thin line, each man ready to flop at the first untoward motion, we edged cautiously nearer. Nothing happened. Nearer again. Still nothing happened. In this tricky manner we came well beneath the huge branches and close to the trunk. From the tree or its bark oozed a strange fragrance halfway between pineapple and cinnamon. The elusive throbbing we'd heard before now sounded more strongly than ever.

It was an imposing tree. Its dark green, fibrous-barked trunk, seven or eight feet in diameter, soared up to twenty-five feet before it began to throw out strong, lengthy branches each of which terminated in one great spatulate leaf. Looking at that massive trunk it was difficult to determine how our quarry had fled up it, but he'd performed the feat like an adept.

All the same, we couldn't see him. Carefully we went round and round the tree a dozen or twenty times, gazing up past its big branches through which green light filtered in large mosaic patterns. Not a sign of him. No doubt about it, he must be somewhere up there but he just couldn't be spotted by us. There was no way in which he could have hopped from this tree to its nearest neighbor, neither could he have come to ground again unobserved. Our collective view of this lump of alien timber was pretty good despite the peculiar, unearthly light, but the more we stared the more invisible he remained.

"This is a prime puzzler!" Stepping well away from the trunk, Jepson sought a better angle of view.

With a mighty *swoosh!* the branch immediately above his head drove down. I could almost hear the tree's yelp of triumph as the swipe gave a boost to my imagination.

The spatulate leaf smacked Jepson squarely across his back and a waft of the pineapple-cinnamon smell went all over the place. Just as swiftly the branch swung up to its original position, taking the victim with it. Roaring with fury, Jepson soared with the leaf and struggled furiously while we gathered in a dumbfounded bunch below. We could see that he was stuck to the underside of that leaf and slowly becoming covered in thick, yellowy-green goo as he writhed madly around. That stuff must have been a hundred times stickier than the best bird-lime.

Together we roared at him to keep still before he got the deadly junk smeared over his face. We had to use a large dollop of decibels and some shameful invective to force his attention. Already his clothes had become covered with goo and his left arm was fastened to his side. He looked a mess. It was obvious that if he got any of it over his mouth and nostrils he'd remain up there and quietly suffocate.

Molders had a determined try at climbing the trunk and found it impossible. He edged away to have a look upward, came hurriedly inward when he noticed another leaf strategically placed to give him a dose of the same.

The safest place was beneath the unfortunate Jepson. Something over twenty feet up, the goo was now crawling slowly over its prey and I estimated that in half an hour he'd be completely covered—in much less if he wriggled around. All this time the dull pulsations continued as though sonorously counting the last moments of the doomed. They made me think of jungle drums heard through thick walls.

Gesturing toward the golden cylinder that was the *Marathon* lying five hundred yards away in the glade, Wilson said, "The more time we waste the worse it's going to be. Let's beat it back, get ropes and steel dogs. We'll soon bring him down."

"No," I decided. "We'll get him a darned sight faster than that."

I stamped around a few times to check the springiness and cushioning qualities of the stuff underfoot. Satisfied, I aimed my needle-ray at the point where Jepson's leaf joined the end of its branch.

Watching me, he let out a bellow of, "Lay off, you crackbrained moron! You'll have me——"

The needler's beam lanced forth at full strength. The leaf dropped off and the tree went mad. Jepson fell twenty-five feet at the incredible rate of two vulgar adjectives per foot. The leaf still fastened to his back, he landed in the undergrowth with a wild yelp and a flood of lurid afterthoughts. While we all lay flat and frantically tried to bury ourselves still deeper, the tree thrashed violently around, its gum-laden spatulates thirsting for vengeance.

One persistent branch kept beating its leaf within a yard of my head as I tried to shove said turnip below ground. I could feel the waft of it coming with rhythmic regularity and sense the pineapple-cinnamon smell permeating the air. It made me sweat to think how my lungs would strain, my eyes pop and my heart burst if I got a generous portion of that junk slapped across my face. I would far rather be needled.

After a while the tree ceased its insane larruping, stood like a dreaming giant liable to go into another frenzy at any moment. Crawling on hands and knees to Jepson, we managed to drag him out of reach, pulling him along on the leaf to which he was fastened.

He couldn't walk, his jackboots and the legs of his pants being firmly glued together. His left arm was just as securely gummed to his side. He was in an awful pickle and complained steadily without pause for breath or thought. Before this happening we had never suspected him of such fluency. But we got him into the safety of the open glade and it was there I recited the few words he'd failed to mention.

Typically stolid, Molders said nothing, contenting him-

93

self with listening to Jepson and me. Molders had helped me do the dragging and now neither of us could let go. We'd become fixed to the original victim, bonded like brothers but not talking like brothers, nor full of anything resembling brotherly love.

So we could do nothing but carry Jepson bodily, with our hands sealed to the most inconvenient parts of his anatomy. This meant he had to be borne horizontally and face downward, like a drunken sailor being frog-marched back to ship. He was still adorned with the leaf.

The task wasn't made any easier or more enjoyable by that young fool Wilson who thought there was something funny in other people's misfortunes. He followed us tee-heeing and steadily snapping his accursed camera which I could have stuffed down his gullet with the greatest pleasure. He was indecently happy at having no goo on himself.

Jay Score, Brennand, Armstrong, Petersen and Drake met us as we lumbered awkwardly across the sward. They stared curiously at Jepson, listened to him with much respect. We warned them not to touch. The pair of us were far from sprightly by the time we reached the *Marathon*. Jepson's weight was only two-thirds normal but after five hundred yards he seemed like the last remains of a glutinous mammoth.

We dumped him on the grass below the open airlock, perforce sitting with him. The faint booming sound continued to throb out of the forest. Jay went into the ship, brought out Sam and Wally to see what they could do about the super-adhesive. The stuff had stiffened and grown hard by now. My hands and fingers felt as though they'd been set into glassite gloves.

Sam and Wally tried cold water, luke-warm water, fairly hot water and very hot water, but none of it did any good. Chief Engineer Douglas had a try with a bottle of rocket-fuel which he frequently used for removing stains, polishing brasses, killing bugs and as a vapour-rub to relieve his lumbago. It could do eighteen other things, too—according to him. But it couldn't dissolve goo.

Next they tried some specially refined gasoline which Steve Gregory keeps for the crew's cigarette lighters. They wasted their time. That gasoline could eat up rubber and one or two other things, but not this stuff. Molders sat blue-eyed and placid, his hands fastened in yellow-green glass.

"You sure are in a fix," said Wilson, with false sympathy. "By gum!"

Sam reappeared with iodine. It didn't work but it did cause a queer foaming on the surface of the adhesive and made a terrible stench. Molders permitted his face to look slightly pained. Some diluted nitric acid brought bubbles on the surface of the hard goo but achieved no more than that. It was risky stuff to use, anyway.

Frowning to himself, Sam went back to look for some other possible solvent, passed Jay Score coming out to see how we were doing. Jay stumbled as he got near to us, a very strange thing for him to do considering his super-human sense of balance. His solid bulk accidentally nudged young Wilson between the shoulder blades and that grinning ape promptly flopped against Jepson's legs where the goo must have remained soft enough to catch hold.

Wilson struggled, started to tie himself up in it, changed his tune when he found it futile. Jepson gave him the sardonic ha-ha as fair swap for a look of sudden death.

Picking up the dropped camera, Jay dangled it from one powerful hand, said with dead-pan contriteness, "I never missed a step before. It was most unfortunate."

"Unfortunate, nothing!" bawled Wilson, wishing Jay would melt down to a tin puddle.

Just then Sam returned bearing a big glass jar, dribbled some of its contents over my imprisoned hands, the sickly green coating at once thinned to a weak slime and my mitts came free.

"Ammonia," remarked Sam. He need not have told me: I could smell the pungent stuff. It was an excellent solvent and he soon had us cleaned up.

Then I chased Wilson three times round the ship. He had the advantage of fewer years and was too fast for me. I gave up the pursuit, breathless. We were about to go aboard and tell our tale to the skipper when that tree started threshing again. You could see its deadly branches beating the air and hear the violent *swoosh!* of them even from this distance. Pausing beneath the airlock we studied

95

the spectacle wonderingly. Then Jay Score spoke, his tones harsh, metallic.

"Where's Kli Yang?"

None of us knew. Now I came to think of it, I couldn't recall him being with us as we dragged Jepson home. The last I remembered of him was when he stood beside me right under that tree and his saucer eyes gave me the creeps by carefully scanning two opposite branches at once.

Armstrong dived into the ship, came out with the report that Kli Yang definitely wasn't among those present. His own eyes as bulgy as the missing Martian's, young Wilson said he couldn't recall Kli Yang coming out of the forest. Upon which we snatched our needlers and made for that tree on the run. All the while it continued to larrup around like a crazy thing tied down by its own roots.

Reaching the monstrous growth, we made a circle just beyond the sweep of its leaves, had a look to see where the Martian was enveloped with glue.

He wasn't.

We discovered him forty feet up the trunk, five of his powerful tentacles clamped around its girth, the other five embracing the green native. The captive struggled wildly and futilely, all the time yelling a high-pitched scream of gibberish.

Carefully Kli Yang edged down the trunk. The way he looked and moved made him resemble an impossible cross between a college professor and an educated octopus. His eyes rolling with terror, the native battered at Kli's head-and-shoulder harness. Kli blandly ignored this hostility, reached the branch that had trapped Jepson, didn't descend any further. Retaining a tight hold on the furiously objecting green one, he crept along the whipping limb until he reached its leafless end. At that point he and the native were being waved up and down in twenty-foot arcs.

Timing himself, he cast off at the lowermost point of one downward sweep, scuttled out of reach before another vengeful branch could swat him. Came a singing howl from a near part of the forest and something vaguely like a blue-green coconut soared out on the shadows and broke at Drake's feet. The queer missile was as thin and brittle as an empty eggshell, had a white inner surface and apparently contained nothing whatever. Taking no notice of the howls or the bomb that wasn't a bomb, Kli Yang bore his still struggling captive toward the *Marathon.*

Drake hung back a moment, had a curious look at the coconut or whatever it was, contemptuously kicked its fragment of shell with his boot. At the same time he caught the full benefit of something floating invisibly from the splinters, sucked in his cheeks, screwed up his eyes and backed away fast. Then he retched. He did it with such violence that he fell over as he retreated. We had the sense to pick him up and rush him after Kli Yang without getting too nosey about what had bitten him. He continued to regurgitate all the way across the grass, recovered only when we came under the ship's bulging side.

"Holy smoke!" he wheezed, nursing his middle. "What an abominable stench. It'd make a skunk smell like the rose of the animal world!" He wiped his lips. "It made my stomach turn right over."

We went to see Kli Yang, whose captive now had been conducted to the galley for a peace-making feed. Dragging off his helmet, Kli said, "That tree wasn't so difficult to mount. It walloped around as I went up but couldn't get at anything on its own trunk." He sniffed with displeasure, rubbed his flat, Red Planet face with the flexible tip of a great tentacle. "Don't know how you primitive bipeds can swallow this soup you call air. I could swim!"

"Where did you find the greenie, Kli?" asked Brennand.

"He was stuck to the trunk more than forty feet up. His entire front fitted perfectly into an indentation in the bark, and his back matched the fibrous trunk so well that I couldn't see him until he moved uneasily as I got close." He picked up the helmet. "A most remarkable example of natural camouflage." Using one eye to look at his helmet, he fixed the other on the interested Brennand, made a gesture of disgust. "How about pulling down the pressure someplace where higher forms of life can live in peace and comfort?"

"We'll pump out the port lock," Brennand promised.

"And don't be so high and mighty with me, you outsize caricature of a rubber spider."

"Bah!" retorted Kli Yang, with great dignity. "Who invented chess yet cannot tell a white pawn from a black rook? Who can't even play duck-on-the-rock without grabbing a load of grief?" With this reference to Terrestrial inexpertness, he slapped his helmet on again and gestured to me to pump it down, which I did. "Thanks!" he said through the diaphragm.

Now to find out something about the greenie.

Captain McNulty himself interviewed the native. The boss sat grandly behind his metal desk, eyed the jittery captive with a mixture of pomposity and kindliness. The native stood before him, his black eyes jerking around with sheer fright. At this close range I could see that he wore a loin-cloth matching his skin. His back was several shades darker than his front, coarser, more fibrous, with little nodules here and there—perfect simulation of the surface of the tree-trunk on which he had sought refuge. Even his loin-cloth was darker at the back than the front. His feet were broad and unshod, the toes double-jointed and as long as the fingers of his hands. Except for the loincloth he was completely naked and had no weapons. The peculiar chrysanthemum on his chest attracted general attention.

"Has he eaten?" asked the skipper, full of solicitude.

"He was offered a meal," Jay told him. "He refused it. He wouldn't touch it. As far as I can make out, all he wants is to get back to his tree."

"Hm-m-m," grunted McNulty. "All in good time." Assuming the expression of a benevolent uncle, he said to the native, "What is your name?"

Grasping the note of interrogation, the green one waved his arms, broke into an untranslatable tirade. On and on and on he went, helping his gabble with many emphatic but incomprehensible gestures. His language was liquid, his voice singsong.

"I see," murmured McNulty as the flood of talk petered out. He blinked inquiringly at Jay Score. "Do you suppose this fellow might be telepathic, like those lobster-things were?"

98

"It is much to be doubted. I'd put him at the mental level of a Congo pygmy—and maybe lower. He doesn't possess so much as a simple spear, let alone bow and arrow or a blowgun."

"I think you're right. His intelligence doesn't seem in any way remarkable." Still maintaining his soothing paternal air, McNulty went on, "There's no common basis on which we can gain his understanding at this stage, so I guess we'll have to create one. We'll dig up our best linguist, set him to learning the rudiments of this fellow's language and teach him some of ours."

"Let me have a try," Jay suggested. "I have the advantage of a mechanical memory."

He lumbered nearer the green native, his huge, well-proportioned body moving silently on the sponge-rubber cushions of his feet. The native didn't like his size nor his quietness, neither did he approve of those brightly lit eyes. He edged away from Jay, edged right to the wall, his optics darting hither and thither as vainly he sought an avenue of escape.

Ceasing his approach as he noted the other's fear, Jay slapped his own head with a hand that could have knocked mine clean off my neck. "Head," he said. He did it half a dozen times, and repeated, "Head, head!"

The green one couldn't have been so stupid; he caught on, faltered, *"Mah."*

Touching his own bean again, Jay inquired, *"Mah?"*

"Bya!" lilted the other, starting to regain his composure.

"See, it's dead easy," approved McNulty, beginning to fancy his own linguistic abilities. *"Mah*—head; *bya*—yes."

"Not necessarily," Jay contradicted. "It all depends upon how his mind translated my action. *Mah* might mean head, face, skull, man, hair, god, mind, thought, or alien, or even the colour black. If he's thinking of my hair as contrasted with his own then *mah* probably does mean black while *bya* may mean not yes, but green."

"Oh, I hadn't thought of that." The skipper looked crushed.

"We'll have to carry on with this performance until we've picked up enough words to form structurally simple

99

sentences. Then we should be able to deduce further meanings from contexts. Give me two or three days."

"Go ahead, then. Do your best, Jay. We can't expect to be able to talk turkey in the first five minutes—it isn't reasonable."

Taking the captive to the rest-room, Jay summoned Minshull and Petersen. He thought three might as well learn something as one. Minshull and Peterson both excelled at languages, speaking Ido, Esperanto, Venusian, high Martian and low Martian—especially low. They were the only ones aboard the ship who gave the chess-maniacs a boiling in their own jargon.

I found Sam in the armoury waiting to hand in the stuff he'd taken out, and I asked, "What did you see from the lifeboat, Sam?"

"Not so much. We weren't out long enough. Didn't get more than a hundred and twenty miles away. Forest, forest, nothing but forest with a few glades scattered here and there. A couple of the glades were large, the size of counties. The biggest in view lay at the end of a long blue lake. We saw several rivers and streams."

"Any signs of superior life?"

"None." He gestured down the passage toward the rest-room where Jay and the others were cross-examining the native, or trying to. "It seems that there must be higher life but you can detect no signs of it from above. Everything remains hidden under thick foliage. Wilson is processing his reel in the hope of finding something our eyes missed. I doubt whether his camera caught anything remarkable."

"Oh, well," I shrugged, "One hundred twenty miles in one direction is nothing by which to estimate an entire world. I don't let myself be deluded, not since that drummer sold me a can of striped paint."

"Didn't it come out?"

"I laid it wrong side up," I told him.

It was right in the middle of that hoary banter that a powerful idea smote me. Following Sam out of the armoury, I made a rush for the radio-room. Steve Gregory sat by his instruments and tried to look busy doing nothing. I was all set to paralyse him with the sheer brilliance of my brainwave.

As Steve cocked an eyebrow at me, I said, "Hey, how about combing the wave-bands?"

"How about combing your hair?" he gave me, frowning.

"My hair is nit and tiddy," I retorted. "Remember those weird whistles and waterfalls we picked up on Mechanistria? Well, if there are any high-lifes on this ball of dirt they may know how to make noises. They'd radiate and you could detect it."

"Sure." He kept his bushy eyebrows still for once, but spoiled it by wiggling his large ears. "*If* they were radiating."

"Then why not go ahead and find out? It would tell us something. What're you waiting for?"

"Look," he said, somewhat deliberately, "have you kept the needlers cleaned, charged and ready for action?"

I stared at him. "You bet I have. They're always ready. That's my job."

"And this one's mine!" He waved the ears again. "You are approximately four hours behind the times. I scoured the ether right after we landed, found nothing but a faint, unmodulated hiss on twelve point three metres. That is Rigel's characteristic discharge and it came from the same direction. D'you think I'm like that snake-armored snorer Sug Farn?"

"No, I don't. Sorry, Steve—it just struck me as a bright idea."

"Oh, it's all right, sergeant," he said amiably. "Every man to his job and every tail-mechanic to his dirt." Idly he twiddled the dials of his slow-motion selectors.

The loudspeaker coughed as if clearing its throat and announced in sharp tones, "*Pip-pip-whop! Pip-pip-whop!*"

Nothing could have been better calculated to upset the determined serenity of his brows. I'll swear that after they'd climbed into his hair they continued over the top, down the back and lodged someplace under his collar.

"Morse," he said in the complaining tone of a hurt child.

"I always thought Morse was an earth-code, not an alien code," I commented. "Anyway, if it is Morse you'll be able to translate it." I paused while the loudspeaker

101

shouted me down with, *"Pip-pipper-pee-eep-whop!"* then concluded, "Every cat to its ash-can."

" 'Tain't Morse," he contradicted himself. "But it's spark signals." He might have frowned if it hadn't taken too long to drag the eyebrows back to his face. Giving me one of those tragic looks you get sometimes, he snatched a pad and started recording the impulses.

The spacesuits, pom-pom chargers and other things had to be serviced, so I left him, returned to the armoury, carried on with my own work. He was still fiddling around when darkness fell. So were Jay and his gang, but not for long.

The sun went down, its long, greenish streamers gradually fading from the sky. A velvet pall came over the forest and glade. I was ambling along the passage toward the galley and near the rest-room when its door jerked open and the green native burst out. His face expressed desperation, his legs were moving as if there were a thousand international smackers tied to the winning tape.

Minshull yelped back in the room as the native went full tilt into my arms. The greenie squirmed like an eel, beat at my features, used his bare feet to try to kick my legs off my torso. His rough, harsh body exuded a weak odour of pineapple-cinnamon.

The others came out at the run, got him tight, talked to him in halting words until he relaxed at least a little. His shifty eyes full of anxiety, he jabbered excitedly at Jay Score, making urgent gestures and waving his woody arms around in a way that reminded me of branches beating the air. Jay managed to soothe him with fair if faltering speech. They had picked up enough words to get along though not enough for perfect understanding. Still, they were managing, after a fashion.

Eventually Jay said to Petersen, "I think you'd better tell the skipper that I want to let Kala go."

Petersen cleared off, returned in a minute. "He says do whatever you think is best."

"Good." Conducting the native to the opening in the starboard lock, Jay yapped at him briefly and gave him the sweet release. The greenie didn't need any second telling; he dived off the rim. Someone in the dark forest must have owed him for a loincloth because his feet made swift brushing sounds as if he fled across the turf like one who has only seconds to spare. Jay stood framed by the rim, his glowing orbs staring into outer gloom.

"Why open the cage, Jay?"

Turning, his said to me, "I've tried to persuade him to come back at sunrise. He may or he may not—it remains to be seen. We didn't have much time to get much out of him, but his language is exceedingly simple and we picked up enough of it to learn that he calls himself Kala of the tribe of Ka. All members of his group are named Ka-something, such as Kalee, Ka'noo, or Ka-heer."

"Like the Martians with their Klis, Leids and Sugs."

"Yes," he agreed, not caring what the Martains might think of being compared with the green aborigines. He also told us that every man has his tree and every gnat its lichen. I don't understand what he means by that, but he satisfied me that in some mysterious manner his life depended upon him being with his tree during darkness. It was imperative. I tried to delay him but his need was pitiful. He preferred to die rather than be away from his tree."

"Sounds silly to me." I blew my nose, grinned at a passing thought. "It would sound far sillier to Jepson."

Jay stared thoughtfully into the deep murkiness from which came strange nocturnal scents and those everlasting pulsations suggestive of muted drums.

"We also learned that there are others in the dark, others mightier than the Ka. They have much *gamish*."

"They have what?" I inquired.

"Much *gamish*," he repeated. "That word defeated me. He used it again and again. He said that the *Marathon* has much *gamish*. I have much *gamish*, and Kli Yang has much *gamish*. Captain McNulty, it appears, has only a little. The Ka have none at all."

"Is it something of which he's afraid?"

"Not exactly. He views it with awe rather than fear. As far as I can make out, anything unusual or surprising or unique is chockful of *gamish*. Anything merely abnormal has a lesser amount of *gamish*. Anything ordinary has none whatever."

"This goes to show the difficulties of communication. It isn't as easy as people back home think it ought to be."

"No, it isn't." His gleaming optics shifted to Armstrong who was leaning against the pom-pom. "Are you doing this guard?"

"Until midnight, then Kelly takes over."

Picking Kelly for guard struck me as poor psychology. That tattooed specimen was permanently attached to a four-foot spanner and in any crisis was likely to wield said instrument in preference to such newfangled articles as pom-poms and needlers. Rumour insisted that he had clung to the lump of iron at his own wedding and that his wife was trying for a divorce based on the thing's effect on her morale. My private opinion was that Kelly was a Neanderthal misplaced in time by many centuries.

"We'll play safe and fasten the lock," decided Jay, "fresh air or no fresh air."

That was characteristic of him and what made him seem so thoroughly human—he could mention fresh air for all the world as if he used it himself. The casual way he did it made you forget that he'd never taken a real breath since the day old Knud Johannsen stood him on his feet and gave him animation.

"Let's plug-in the turnscrew."

Turning his back upon the throbbing dark, he started to walk into the lighted airlock, treading carefully along the cutout through the threads.

A piping voice came out of the night and ejaculated, *"Nou baiders!"*

Jay halted in mid-step. Feet padded outside just underneath the lock's opening. Something spherical and glassy soared through the worm, skidded over Jay's left shoulder, broke to shards on the top recoil chamber of the pom-pom. A thin, golden and highly volatile liquid splashed out of it and vapourised instantly.

Reversing on one heel, Jay faced the black opening. The startled Armstrong made a jump to the wall, put out a thumb to jab the stud of the general alarm. He didn't make it. Without touching the stud he went down as though slugged by someone invisible.

My needler out, its muzzle extended, I moved cautiously forward, saw the glittering thread of the worm making metallic rings around the picture of Jay posing against the ebony background. It was a mistake; I ought to have had a stab at that stud.

Three steps and the stuff from that busted bottle got me the same way as it had caught Armstrong. The picture of Jay swelled like a blown bubble, the circle widened, grew enormous, the threads of the worm became broad and deep with Jay as a gigantic figure standing in the middle of them. The bubble burst and I went down with my mind awhirl and fading away.

Don't know how long I remained corpselike, for when I eventually opened my eyes it was with the faint uncertain memory of hearing much shouting and stamping of feet around my prostrate form. Things must have happened over and all around me while I lay like so much discarded meat. Now I was still flat. I reposed full length on deep, dew-soaked turf with the throbbing forest close on my left, the indifferent stars peering down from the vault of night. I was bound like an Egyptian mummy. Jepson made another mummy at one side, Armstrong at the other. Several more reposed beyond them.

Three or four hundred yards away angry noises were spoiling the silence of the dark, a mixture of Terrestial oaths and queer, alien pipings. The *Marathon* lay that way; all that could be seen of her was the funnel of light pouring from her open lock. The light flickered, waxed and waned, once or twice was momentarily obliterated. Evidently a struggle was taking place in the shaft of light which became blocked as the fight swayed to and fro.

Jepson snored as though it were Sunday afternoon in the old home town, but Armstrong had recovered the use of his wits and tongue. He employed both with vigour and imagination. Rolling over, he started chewing at Blaine's bindings. A vaguely human-looking shape came silently from the darkness and smote downward. Armstrong went quiet.

Blinking my eyes, I adapted them sufficiently to discern several more shapes standing around half-hidden in the bad light. Keeping still and behaving myself, I thought uncomplimentary thoughts about McNulty, the *Marathon*, old Flottnor who invented the ship, plus all the public spirited folk who'd backed him morally and financially. I'd often had the feeling that sooner or later they'd be the death of me and now it seemed that said feeling was going to prove justified.

Deep down inside a tiny, nagging voice said, "Sergeant, do you remember that promise you made your mother about bad language? Do you remember that time you gave a Venusian guppy a can of condensed milk in exchange for a pinfire opal not as big as the city clock? Repent, sergeant, while yet there is time!"

So I laid in peace and did a bit of vain regretting. Over there by the intermittent light-shaft the pipings rose crescendo and the few earthly voices died away. There sounded occasional smashings of fragile, brittle things. More dim shapes brought more bodies, dumped them nearby and melted back into the gloom. I wish I could have counted the catch but darkness wouldn't permit it. All the newcomers were unconscious but revived rapidly. I could recognize Brennand's angry voice and the skipper's asthmatic breathing.

A cold blue star shone through a thin fringe of drifting clouds as the fight ended. The succeeding pause was ghastly: a solemn, brooding silence broken only by a faint scuffle of many naked feet in the grass, and by the steady booming in the forest.

Forms gathered around in large numbers. The glade was full of them. Hands lifted me, tested my bonds, tossed me into a wicker hammock and I was borne along shoulder-high. I felt like a defunct warthog being toted in some hunter's line of native porters. Just meat—that was me. Just a trophy of the chase. I wondered whether God would confront me with that guppy.

The caravan filed into the forest, my direction of progress being head-first. Another hammock followed immediately behind and I could sense rather than see a string of them farther back.

Jepson was the sardine following me; he went horizontally along making a loud recitation about how he'd been tied up ever since he landed in this world. Not knowing the astronomer who had selected this planet for investigation, he identified him by giving him a name in which no man would take pride and embellished it with a long series of fanciful and vulgar titles.

Curving warily around one semivisible tree, our line marched boldly under the next, dodged the third and fourth. How they could tell one growth from another in this lousy light was beyond my comprehension.

We had just come deeply into the deepest darkness when a tremendous explosion sounded way back in the glade and a column of fire lit up the sky. Even the fire looked faintly green. Our line halted. Two or three hundred voices cheeped querulously, starting from the front and going past me to a hundred yards farther back.

"They've blown up the *Marathon*," thought I. "Oh, well, all things come to an end, including the flimsiest hope of returning home."

Surrounding cheeping and piping became drowned out as the noisy pillar of flame built itself up to an earth-shaking roar. My hammock tilted and swayed while those holding it reacted in alarm. The way they put on the pace had to be experienced to be believed; I almost flew along, avoiding one tree but not another, sometimes turning at safe distance from unseen growths that were not trees at all. My heart lay down in my boots.

The bellowing in the glade suddenly ended in a mighty thump and a crimson spear flung itself into the sky and stabbed through the clouds. It was a spectacle I'd seen many a time before but had thought never to see again. A space-ship going up! It was the *Marathon!*

Were these alien creatures so talented that they could grab a thoroughly strange vessel, quickly understand its workings and take it wherever they wanted? Were these the beings described as superior to the Ka? The whole situation struck me as too incongruous for belief: expert astronauts carrying prisoners in primitive wicker hammocks. Besides, the agitated way in which they'd jabbered and put on the pace suggested that the *Marathon's* spectacular spurt of life had taken them by surprise. The mystery was one I couldn't solve nohow.

While the fiery trail of the ship arced northward our party hurriedly pressed on. There was one stop during which our captors congregated together, but their continual piping showed that they had not halted for a meal.

Twenty minutes later there came a brief hold-up and a first-class row up front. Guards kept close to us while a short distance ahead sounded a vocal uproar in which many voices vied with a loud mewing and much beating of great branches. I tried to imagine a bright green tiger.

Things went phut-phut like fat darts plonking into wet leather. The mewing shot up to a squeal then ended in a choking cough. We moved on, making a wide bend around a monstrous growth that I strove in vain to see. If only this world had possessed a moon. But there wasn't a moon; only the stars and the clouds and the menacing forest from which came that all-pervading beat, beat, beat.

Dawn broke as the line warily dodged a small clump of apparently innocent saplings. We arrived at the bank of a wide river. Here, for the first time, we could give our guards a close examination as they shepherded burdens and bearers down the bank.

These were creatures very much like the Ka, only taller, more slender, with large intelligent eyes. They had similarly fibrous skins, grayer, not so green, and the same chrysanthemums on their chests. Unlike the Ka, their middles were clothed in pleated garments, they had harnesses of woven fibre, plus various wooden accoutrements like complicated blow-guns and bowl-shaped vessels having a bulbous container in the base. A few also bore small panniers holding glassy spheres like the one that had laid me flat in the airlock.

Craning my head I tried to see more but could discern only Jepson in the next hammock and Brennand in the one behind that. The next instant, mine was unceremoniously dumped by the water's brink, Jepson's alongside me, the rest in a level row.

Turning his face toward me, Jepson said, "The smelly bums!"

"Take it easy," I advised. "If we play it their way they may give us more rope."

"And," he went on, viciously, "I don't care for guys who try to be witty at the wrong time."

"I wasn't trying to be witty," I snapped back. "We're bound to hold our own opinions, aren't we? You're all tied up."

"There you go again!" He did some furious writhing around and strove to stretch his fastenings. "Some day I'll tie you, and for keeps!"

I didn't answer. No use wasting breath on a man in a bad mood. Daylight waxed stronger, penetrating the thin green mist hanging over the green river. I could now see Blaine and Minshull supine beyond Armstrong and the portly form of McNulty beyond them.

Ten of our captors went along the line opening jackets and shirts, baring our chests. They had with them a supply of the bowls with bulbous containers. A pair of them pawed my uniform apart, got my chest exposed, and stared at it. Something about my bosom struck them as wonderful beyond the power of telling, and it wasn't the spare beard I kept there.

It didn't require overmuch brains to guess that they missed my chrysanthemum and couldn't figure how I'd got through life without it. Calling their fellows, the entire gang debated the subject while I lay bared before them like a sacrificial lamb. Finally they decided that they had struck a new and absorbing line of research and went hot along the trail.

Seizing Blaine and the boob who'd played duck-on-the-rock, they untied them, stripped them down to the raw, studied them like prize cattle at an agricultural exhibition. One of them prodded Blaine in the solar plexus where his whatzis ought to have been, whereat he jumped on the fellow with a savage whoop and brought him down. The other nudist promptly grabbed the opportunity to join in. Armstrong, who never had been a ninety pound weakling, made a mighty effort, burst his bonds, came up dark-faced with the strain and roared into the fray. Fragments of his mangled hammock swung and bounced on his beefy back.

All along the line we made violent attempts to burst out of bonds but without avail. Green ones centred on the scene of the struggle, brittle spheres plopped all around the three fighting Earthmen. The tail-mechanic and Blaine collapsed together. Armstrong shuddered and bawled, teetered and pulled himself together, held out long enough to toss two natives into the river and slug the daylights out of a third. Then he too went down.

Dragging their fellows from the river, the green ones dressed the slumber-wrapped Blaine and the other, added Armstrong, securely tied all three. Once more they conferred. I couldn't make head or tail of their canary-talk but conceived the notion that in their opinion we had an uncertain quantity of *gamish*.

My bonds began to irk. I'd have given a lot for the chance to go into action and bash a few green heads. Twisting myself, I used a lacklustre eye to study a tiny shrub growing near the side of my hammock. The shrub jiggled its midget branches and emitted a smell of burned caramel. Local vegetation was all movement and stinks.

Abruptly the green ones ended their talk, crowded down the bank of the river. A flotilla of long, narrow, shapely vessels swept round the bend, foamed in to the bank. We were carted on board, five prisoners per boat. Thrusting away from the bank, our crew of twenty pulled and pushed rhythmically at a row of ten wooden levers on each side of the boat, drove the vessel upstream at fair pace and left a narrow wake on the river's surface.

"I had a grandfather who was a missionary," I told Jepson. "He got into trouble of this kind."

"So what?"

"He went to pot," I said.

"I sincerely hope you do likewise," offered Jepson, without charity. He strained futilely at his bindings.

For lack of anything better to occupy my attention I watched the way in which our crew handled their vessel, came to the conclusion that the levers worked two large pumps or maybe a battery of small ones, and that the vessel made progress by sucking water in at the bow and squirting it out at the stern.

Later, I found I was wrong. Their method was much simpler than that. The levers connected under water with twenty split-bladed paddles. The two flaps of each blade closed together on one stroke, opened on the return stroke. By this means they got along rather faster than they could have done with oars since the subsurface paddles moved forward and back with only their own weight on the boat—they didn't have to be raised, turned and lowered by the muscles of the rowers.

The sun climbed higher while we made way steadily

upriver. At the second bend the waterway split, its current flowing at increased pace on either side of a rocky islet about a hundred yards long. A group of four huge, sinister-looking trees stood at the upstream end of the islet, their trunks and limbs a sombre green verging on black. Each of them bore a horizontal spray of big branches above which the trunk continued to soar to a feathery crest sixty feet higher. Each of these branches ended in half a dozen thick, powerful digits that curved downward like the fingers of a clutching hand.

The crews speeded up their levers to the limit. The string of boats headed into the right-hand channel over which reached the biggest and most menacing of those branches. As the first boat's prow came underneath it, the branch hungrily twitched its fingers. It was no illusion: I saw it as clearly as I see my trip bonus when they slide it toward me across the mahogany. That mighty limb was getting all set to grab and from its size and spread I reckoned it could pluck the entire boatload clean out of the water and do things of which I didn't care to think.

But it didn't do it. Just as that boat came into the danger area its helmsman stood up and yelled a stream of gibberish at the tree. The fingers relaxed. The helmsman of the next boat did the same. And the next. Then mine. Flat on my back, as ready for action as a corpse, I gaped at that enormous neck-wringer while all too slowly it came on, passed above and fell behind. Our helmsman went silent; and the one in the following boat took up the tale. There was dampness down my spine.

Five miles farther on we turned in to the opposite bank. My head was toward that side and I didn't get a view of the buildings until the greenies tossed me out of my hammock, released me from the thing and stood me on my feet. I promptly lost balance and sat down. Temporarily, my dogs were dead. Rubbing them to restore the circulation, my curious eyes examined this dump that might have been anything from a one-horse hamlet to a veritable metropolis.

Its cylindrical buildings were of light green wood, of uniform height and diameter, and each had a big tree growing through its middle. The foliage of each tree extended farther than the radius of each house, thus effectively hiding it from overhead view. Nothing could have been better calculated to conceal the place from the air, though there wasn't any reason to suppose that the inhabitants had cause to fear a menace from above.

Still, the way in which trees and buildings shared the same sites made it quite impossible to estimate the size of the place, for beyond the nearer screen of round houses were trees, trees and still more trees, each one of which may have shielded an alien edifice.

I couldn't tell whether I was looking at a mere kraal or at the riverside suburb of a super-city extending right over the horizon. Little wonder that the exploring lifeboat had observed nothing but forest. Its crew could have scouted over an area holding many millions and thought it nothing but jungle.

Weapons ready, eyes alert, a horde of green ones clustered around us while others finished the task of untying prisoners. The fact that we'd arrived in a miraculous contraption like the *Marathon* didn't seem to impress them one little bit. My feet had become obedient by now. I lugged on my jackboots, stood up and stared around. It was then that I got two shocks.

The first hit me as I made a mental list of my companions in misery. It consisted of little more than half the complement of the *Marathon*. The others weren't there. One hammock held a pale, lax figure I recognised as the body of the guy who'd caught that load of darts soon after we landed. Why the greenies had seen fit to drag a cadaver along I just don't know.

Upon a pair of linked-together hammocks reposed the awake but dreamy and disinterested form of Sug Farn. But he was the only Martian present. None of the rest of the Red Planet mob were there. Neither were Chief Douglas, Bannister, Kane, Richards, Kelly, Jay Score, Steve Gregory, young Wilson and a dozen more.

Were they dead? It didn't seem so, else why should the greenies have transported one body but not the others? Had they escaped? Or did they form a second party of prisoners that had been taken somewhere else? There was no way of determining their fate, yet it was strange that they should be missing.

112

I nudged Jepson. "Hey, have you noticed——?"

A sudden roar over the river cut me off in mid-sentence. All the green ones gaped upward and gesticulated with their weapons. They were making mouth motions but couldn't be heard because the noise drowned what they were saying. Whirling around to take a look, I could feel my own eyes bug out on stalks as the *Marathon's* sleek pinnace dived within a few feet of the river's surface, soared upward again. It vanished over the tree-tops and bellowed into the distance.

But one could still follow the sound of it sweeping round in a great circle. The note screamed higher as it accelerated and went into another dive. Next instant it shot again into view, swooped so low that it touched the water, whisked a shower of green droplets behind it and sent a small wash lapping up the bank. For the second time it disappeared in a swift and ear-racking soar, bulleting past and away at such a pace that it was impossible to tell who was spotting us from the pilot's cabin.

Spitting on his knuckles, Jepson gave the greenies a sour eye. "They've got it coming to them, the lice!"

"Tut!" I chided.

"As for you," he went on. He didn't add more because at that moment a tall, thin, mean-looking greenie picked on him. This one gave him a contemptuous shove in the chest and piped something on a rising note of interrogation. "Don't you do that to me!" snarled Jepson, giving him an answering shove.

The green one staggered backward, taken by surprise. He kicked out his right leg. I thought he was trying to give Jepson a hearty crack on the shins, but he wasn't. The gesture was a good deal deadlier. He was throwing something with his foot and what he threw was alive, superfast and vicious. All I could see of it was a thing that may or may not have been a tiny snake. It had no more length and thickness than a pencil and—for a change— wasn't green, but a bright orange colour relieved by small black spots. It landed on Jepson's chest, bit him, then flicked down his front with such rapidity that I could hardly follow its motion. Reaching the ground, it made the grass faintly whip aside as it streaked back to its master.

Curling around the green one's ankle, it went supine,

looking exactly like a harmless leg ornament. A very small number of other natives wore similar objects all of which were black and orange except one that was yellow and black.

The attacked Jepson bulged his eyes, opened his mouth but produced no sound though obviously trying. He teetered. The native wearing the yellow and black lump of wickedness stood right by my side studying Jepson with academic interest.

I broke his neck.

The way it snapped reminded me of a rotten broomstick.

This thing on his leg deserted him the moment he became mutton, but fast as it moved it was too late. I was ready for it this time. Jepson fell on his face just as my jackboot crunched the pseudosnake into the turf.

A prime hullabaloo was going on all around. I could hear McNulty's anxious voice shouting, "Men! Men!" Even at a time like this the overly conscientious crackpot could dwell on visions of himself being demoted for tolerating ill-treatment of natives.

Armstrong kept bawling, "One more!" and each time there had followed a loud splash in the river. Blow-guns were going *phut-phut* and spheres breaking right and left. Jepson lay like one dead while combatants milled over his body. Brennand barged up against me. He breathed in long, laboured gasps and was doing his utmost to gouge the eyes out of a green face.

By this time I'd helped myself to another aborigine and proceeded to take him apart. I tried to imagine that he was a fried chicken of which I never seem to get any more than the piece that goes last over a fence. He was hard to hold, this greenie, and bounced around like a rubber ball. Over his swaying shoulders I caught a glimpse of Sug Farn juggling five at once and envied him the bunch of anacondas he used for limbs. My opponent stabbed hostile fingers into the chrysanthemum I didn't possess, looked surprised at his own forgetfulness, was still trying to think up some alternative method of incapacitating me as he went into the river.

114

Now several spheres cracked open at my feet and the last I remember hearing was Armstrong releasing a bellow of triumph just before a big splash. The last I remember seeing was Sug Farn suddenly shooting out a spare tentacle he'd temporarily overlooked and using it to arrange that of the six greenies who were jumping on me only five landed. The other one was still going up as I went down.

For some reason I didn't pass out as completely as I'd done before. Maybe I got only a half-dose of whatever the spheres gave forth, or perhaps they contained a different and less positive mixture. All that I know is that I dropped with five natives astride my ribs, the skies spun crazily, my brains turned to cold and lumpy porridge. Then, astonishingly, I was wide awake, my upper limbs again tightly bound.

Over to the left a group of natives formed a heaving pile atop some forms that I couldn't see but could easily hear. Armstrong did some champion hog-calling underneath that bunch which—after a couple of hectic minutes —broke apart to reveal his pinioned body along with those of Blaine and Sug Farn. On my right lay Jepson, his limbs quite free but the lower ones apparently helpless. There was now no sign of the pinnace, no faraway moaning to show that it was still airborne.

Without further ado the greenies whisked us across the sward and five miles deep into the forest, or city, or whatever it ought to be called. Two of them bore Jepson in a wicker hamper. Even at this inland point there were still as many houses as trees. Here and there a few impassive citizens came to the doors of their abodes and watched us dragging along our way. You'd have thought we were the sole surviving specimens of the dodo from the manner in which they weighed us up.

Minshull and McNulty walked right behind me in this death parade. I hear the latter give forth pontifically, "I shall speak to their leader about this. I'll point out to him that all these unfortunate struggles are the inevitable result of his own people's irrational bellicosity."

"Without a doubt," endorsed Minshull, heartily sardonic.

"Making every possible allowance for mutual difficulty

in understanding," McNulty continued, "I still think we are entitled to be received with a modicum of courtesy."

"Oh, quite," said Minshull. His voice was now solemn, like that of the president of a morticians' convention. "And we consider that our reception leaves much to be desired."

"Precisely my point," approved the skipper.

"Therefore any further hostilities would be most deplorable," added Minshull, with a perfectly dead pan.

"Of course," McNulty enthused.

"Not to mention that they'd compel us to tear the guts out of every green-skinned critter on this stinking planet."

"Eh?" McNulty missed a step, his features horrified. "What was that you just said?"

Minshull looked innocently surprised. "Why, nothing, skipper. I didn't even open my mouth. You must be dreaming things."

What the outraged shipmaster intended to retort to that remained a mystery for at this point a greenie noticed him lagging and prodded him on. With an angry snort he speeded up, moving in introspective silence thereafter.

Presently we emerged from a long, orderly line of tree-shrouded homes and entered a glade fully twice as large as that in which the missing *Marathon* had made its landing. It was roughly circular, its surface level and carpeted with close-growing moss of a rich emerald-green. The sun, now well up in the sky, poured a flood of pale green beams into this alien amphitheatre around the fringes of which clustered a horde of silent, expectant natives, watching us with a thousand eyes.

The middle of the glade captured our attention. Here, as outstanding as the biggest skyscraper in the old home town, towered a veritable monster among trees. How high it went was quite impossible to estimate but it was plenty large enough to make Terra's giant redwoods look puny by comparison. Its bole was nothing less than forty feet in diameter and the spread of its oaklike branches looked immense even though greatly shrunk in perspective way, way up there. So enormous was this mighty growth that we couldn't keep our eyes off it. If these transcosmic Zulus intended to hang us, well, it'd be done high and handsome. Our kicking bodies wouldn't look more than a few struggling bugs suspended between earth and heaven.

Minshull must have been afflicted with similar thoughts, for I heard him say to McNulty, "There's the Christmas tree. We'll be the ornaments. Probably they'll draw lots for us and the boob who gets the ace of spades will select the fairy at the top."

"Don't be morbid," snapped McNulty. "They'll do nothing so illegal."

Then a big, wrinkled-faced native pointed at the positive skipper and six pounced on him before he could dilate further on the subject of interstellar law. With complete disregard for all the customs and rules that the victim held holy, they bore him toward the waiting tree.

Up to that moment we'd failed to notice the drumming sound which thundered dully from all around the glade. It was very strong now, and held a sinister quality in its muffled but insistent beat. The weird, elusive sound had been with us from the start; we'd become used to it, had grown unconscious of it in the same way that one fails to notice the ticking of a familiar clock. But now, perhaps because it lent emphasis to the dramatic scene, we were keenly aware of that deadly *throb-throb-throb*.

The green light made the skipper's face ghastly as he was led forward unresisting. All the same, he still managed to lend importance to his characteristic strut and his features had the ridiculous air of one who nurses unshakable faith in the virtue of sweet reasonableness. I have never encountered a man with more misplaced confidence in written law. As he went forward I know he was supported by the profound conviction that these poor, benighted people were impotent to do anything drastic to him without first filling in the necessary forms and getting them properly stamped and countersigned. Whenever McNulty died, it was going to be with official approval and after all official formalities had been satisfied.

Halfway to the tree the skipper and his escort were met by nine tall natives. Dressed in no way differently from their fellows, these managed to convey in some vague manner that they were beings apart from the common herd. Witch-doctors, decided my agitated mind.

Those holding McNulty promptly handed him over to

the newcomers and beat it toward the fringe of the glade as if the devil himself were due to appear in the middle. There wasn't any devil; only that monstrous tree. But knowing what some growths could and did do in this green-wrapped world it was highly probable that this one—the grandpappy of all trees—was capable of some unique and formidable kind of wickedness. Of that statuesque lump of timber one thing was certain: it possessed more than its fair share of *gamish*.

Briskly the nine stripped McNulty to the waist. He continued talking to them all the time but he was too far away for us to get the gist of his authoritative lecture of which his undressers took not the slightest notice. Again they made close examination of his chest, conferred among themselves, started dragging him nearer to the tree. McNulty resisted with appropriate dignity. They didn't stand on ceremony when he pulled back; picking him up bodily they carried him forward.

Armstrong said in tight tones, "We've still got legs, haven't we?" and forthwith kicked the nearest guard's feet from under him.

But before any of us could follow his example and start another useless fracas an interruption came from the sky. Upon the forest's steady drumming was superimposed another fiercer, more penetrating moan that built up to a rising howl. The howl then changed to an explosive roar as, swift and silvery, the pinnace swooped low over the fateful tree.

Something dropped from the belly of the bulleting boat, blew out to umbrella shape, hesitated in its fall, lowered gently into the head of the tree. A parachute! I could see a figure dangling in the harness just before it was swallowed in the thickness of elevated foliage, but distance made it impossible to identify this arrival from above.

The nine who were carrying McNulty unceremoniously dumped him on the moss, gazed at the tree. Strangely enough, aerial manifestations filled these ʟatives more with curiosity than fear. The tree posed unmoving. Suddenly amid its top branches a needle-ray lanced forth, touched a large branch at its junction with the trunk, severed it. The amputated limb plunged to ground.

At once a thousand budlike protuberances that lay hidden between the leaves of the tree swelled up like blown toy balloons, reached the size of giant pumpkins and burst with a fusillade of dull plops. From them exploded a yellow mist which massed at such a rate and in such quantity that the entire tree became clouded with it in less than a minute.

All the natives within sight hooted like a flock of scared owls, turned and ran. McNulty's nine guardians also abandoned whatever they had in mind and dashed after their fellows. The needler caught two of them before they'd gone ten steps; the other seven doubled their pace. McNulty was left struggling with the bonds around his wrists while slowly the mist crawled toward him.

Again the beam speared high up in the tree. Again a huge branch tumbled earthward. Already the tree had grown dim within the envelope of its own fog. The last native had faded from sight. The creeping yellow vapour had come within thirty yards of the skipper who was standing and staring at it like a man fascinated. His wrists remained tied to his sides. Deep inside the mist the popping sounds continued, though not as rapidly.

Yelling at the witless McNulty to make use of his nether limbs, we struggled furiously with our own and each other's bonds. McNulty's only response was to shuffle backward a few yards. By a superhuman effort, Armstrong burst free, snatched a jacknife from his pants pocket, started cutting our arms loose. Minshull and Blaine, the first two thus relieved, immediately raced to McNulty who was posing within ten yards of the mist like a portly Ajax defying the power of alien gods. They brought him back.

Just as we'd all got rid of our bonds the pinnace came round in another wide sweep, vanished behind the column of yellow cloud and thundered into the distance. We gave it a hoarse cheer. Then from the base of the mist strode a great figure dragging a body by each hand. It was Jay Score. He had a tiny two-way radio clamped on his back.

He came toward us, big, powerful, his eyes shining with their everlasting fires, released his grip on the cadavers, said, "Look—this is what the vapour will do to you unless you move out mighty fast!"

We looked. These bodies belonged to the two natives

119

he'd needled but the needlers had not caused that awful rotting of the flesh. Both leprous objects were too far gone to be corpses, not far enough to be skeletons. Mere rags of flesh and half-dissolved organs on frames of festering bone. It was easy to see what would have happened to Jay had he been composed of the same stuff as ourselves, or had he been an air-breather.

"Back to the river," advised Jay, "even if we have to fight our way through. The *Marathon* is going to land in the glade alongside it. We must reach her at all costs."

"And remember, men," put in McNulty officiously, "I want no unnecessary slaughter."

That was a laugh! Our sole weapons now consisted of Jay's needler, Armstrong's jacknife, and our fists. Behind us, already very near and creeping steadily nearer, was the mist of death. Between us and the river lay the greenie metropolis with its unknown number of inhabitants armed with unknown devices. Veritably we were between a yellow devil and a green sea.

We started off, Jay in the lead, McNulty and the burly Armstrong following. Immediately behind them, two men carried Jepson who could still use his tongue even if not his legs. Two more bore the body which our attackers had brought all the way from the ship. Without opposition or mishap we got a couple of hundred yards into the forest and there we buried the remains of the man who first set foot on this soil. He went from sight with the limp, unprotesting silence of the dead while all around us the jungle throbbed.

In the next hundred yards we were compelled to bury another. The surviving duck-on-the-rock player, sobered by the dismal end of his buddy, took the lead as a form of penance. We were marching slowly and cautiously, our eyes alert for a possible ambush, our wits ready to react to any untoward move by a dart-throwing bush or a geo-smearing branch.

The man in front swerved away from one tree that topped an empty greenie abode. His full attention remained fixed upon the dark entrance to that house and thus he failed to be wary of another tree under which he was moving. Of medium size, this growth had a silvery green bark, long, ornamental leaves from which dangled numerous sprays of stringy threads the ends of which came to within three or four feet of the ground. He brushed against two of the threads. Came a sharp, bluish flash of light, a smell of ozone and scorched hair, and he collapsed. He had been electrocuted as thoroughly as if smitten by a stroke of lightning.

Mist or no mist, we carried him back the hundred yards we'd just traversed, interred him beside his comrade. The job was done in the nick of time; that crawling vaporous leprosy had reached near to our very heels as we resumed our way. High in the almost concealed sky the sun poured down its limpid rays and made mosaic patterns through overhead leaves.

Giving a wide berth to this newest menace, which we dubbed the voltree, we hit the end of what passed for Main Street in these parts. Here we had an advantage in one respect but not in another. The houses stood dead in line and well apart; we could march along the centre of this route beneath the wider gap of sky and be beyond reach of this planet's bellicose vegetation. But this made us so much the more vulnerable to attack from any direction by natives determined to oppose our escape. We would have to do the trip, one way or another, with our necks stuck out a yard.

As we trudged stubbornly ahead, mentally prepared to face whatever might yet come, Sug Farn said to me, "You know, I have an idea well worth developing."

"What is it?" I asked, enjoying a thrill of hopefulness.

"Suppose that we had twelve squares a side," he suggested, blandly ignoring present circumstances, "we could then have four more pawns and four new master pieces per side. I propose to call the latter 'archers'. They would move two squares forward and could take opponents only one square sidewise. Wouldn't that make a beautifully complicated game?"

"I hope you swallow a chess-set and ruin your insides," I said, disappointed.

"As I should have known, your mental appreciation accords with that of the lower vertebrates." So saying, he extracted a bottle of *hooloo* scent which somehow he'd managed to retain through all the ructions, moved away from me and sniffed at it in a calculatingly offensive manner. I don't give a hoot what anybody says—we don't smell like Martians say we do! These snake-armed snoots are downright liars!

Stopping both our progress and argument, Jay Score growled, "I guess this will do." Unlhing his portable radio, he turned it, said into its microphone, "That you, Steve?" A pause, followed by, "Yes, we're waiting about a quarter of a mile on the river side of the glade. There's been no opposition—yet. But it'll come. All right, we'll stay put awhile." Another pause. "Yes, we'll guide you."

Turning his attention from the radio to the sky, but with one earpiece still held to his head, he listened intently. We all listened. For a while we could hear nothing but that *throb-throb-throb* that never ended upon this crazy world, but presently came a faraway drone like the hum of a giant bumble-bee.

Jay picked up the microphone. "We've got you now. You're heading right way and coming nearer." The drone grew louder. "Nearer, nearer." He waited a moment. The drone seemed to drift off at an angle. "Now you're away to one side." Another brief wait. The distant sound suddenly became strong and powerful. "Heading correctly." It swelled to a roar. "Right!" yelled Jay. "You're almost upon us!"

He glanced expectantly upward and we did the same like one man. The next instant the pinnace raced across the sky-gap at such a pace that it had come and gone in less time than it takes to draw a breath. All the same, those aboard must have seen us for the little boat zoomed around in a wide, graceful arc, hit the main stem a couple of miles farther along, came back up it at terrific speed. This time we could watch it all the way and we bawled at it like a gang of excited kids.

"Got us?" inquired Jay of the microphone. "Then make a try on the next run."

Again the pinnace swept round, struck its former path, tore the air as it shot toward us. It resembled a monster shell from some oldtime cannon. Things fell from its underside, bundles and packages in a parachuted stream. The stuff poured down as manna from heaven while the sower passed uproariously on and dug a hole in the northern sky. But for these infernal trees the pinnace could have done even better by landing and snatching the lot of us from danger's grasp.

Eagerly we pounced on the supplies, tearing covers open, dragging out the contents. Spacesuits for all. Well, they'd serve to protect us from various forms of gaseous unpleasantness. Needlers, oiled and loaded, with adequate reserves of excitants. A small case, all sponge rubber and cotton wool, containing half a dozen midget atomic bombs. An ampoule of iodine and a first-aid pack per man.

One large bundle had become lodged high up in the branches of a tree, or rather its parachute had become entangled and left it dangling enticingly by the ropes. Praying that it contained nothing likely to blast the earth from under us, we needled the ropes and brought it down. It proved to hold a large supply of concentrated rations plus a five gallon can of fruit juice.

Packing the chutes and shouldering the supplies, we started off. The first mile proved easy; just trees, trees, trees and houses from which the inhabitants had fled. It was on this part of the journey I noticed it was always the same type of tree that surmounted a house. No abode stood under any of those goo-slappers or electrocuters of whose powers we were grimly aware. Whether these house-trees were innocuous was a question nobody cared to investigate, but it was here that Minshull discovered them as the source of that eternal throbbing.

Disregarding McNulty, who clucked at him like an agitated hen, Minshull tiptoed into one empty house, his needler ready for trouble. A few seconds later he reappeared, said that the building was deserted but that the tree in its centre was booming like a tribal tomtom. He'd put his ear to its trunk and had heard the beating of its mighty heart.

That started a dissertation by McNulty on the subject of our highly questionable right to mutilate or otherwise harm the trees of this planet. If, in fact, they were semi-sentient, then in interstellar law they had the status of aborigines and as such were legally protected by subsection so-and-so, paragraph such-and-such of the Transcosmic Code governing planetary relations. He entered into all legalistic aspects of this matter with much gusto and complete disregard for the fact that he might be boiled in oil before nightfall.

When eventually he paused for breath, Jay Score pointed out, "Skipper, maybe these people have laws of their own and are about to enforce them." He pointed straight ahead.

I followed the line of his finger then frantically poured myself into my spacesuit. The record time for encasing oneself is said to be twenty-seven seconds. I beat it by twenty, but can never prove it. This, I thought, is the pay-off. The long arm of justice was about to face me with that poor guppy and one can of condensed milk.

Awaiting us half a mile ahead was a vanguard of enormous snakelike things far thicker than my body and no less than a hundred feet in length. They writhed in our general direction, their movements peculiarly stiff and lacking sinuosity. Behind them, also moving awkwardly forward, came a small army of bushes deceivingly harmless in appearance. And behind those, hooting with the courage of those who feel themselves secure, was a horde of green natives. The progress of this nightmarish army was determined by the pace of the snakish objects in the lead, and these crept forward in tortuous manner as if striving to move a hundred times faster than was natural.

Aghast at this incredible spectacle, we halted. The creepers came steadily on and somehow managed to convey an irresistible impression of tremendous strength keyed-up for sudden release. The nearer they came, the bigger and nastier they looked. By the time they were a mere three hundred yards away I knew that any one of them could embrace a bunch of six of us and do more to the lot than any boa constructor ever did to a hapless goat.

These were the wild ones of a fast and semisentient forest. I knew it instinctively and I could hear them faintly mewing as they advanced. These, then, were my bright green tigers, samples of the thing our captors had battled in the emerald jungle. But apparently they could be tamed, their strength and fury kept on tap. This tribe had done it. Veritably they were higher than the Ka.

"I think I can just about make this distance," said Jay

Score when the intervening space had shrunk to two hundred yards.

Nonchalantly he thumbed a little bomb that could have made an awful mess of the *Marathon* or a boat twice its size. His chief and most worrying weakness was that he never did appreciate the power of things that go bang. So he carelessly juggled it around in a way that made me wish him someplace the other side of the cosmos and just when I was about to burst into tears, he threw it. His powerful arm also whistled through the air as he flung the missile in a great arc.

We flattened. The earth heaved like the belly of a sick man. Huge clods of plasma and lumps of torn green fibrous stuff geysered high, momentarily hung in mid-air, then showered all around. Getting up, we raced forward a hundred yards, went prone as Jay flung another. This one made me think of volcanoes being born alongside my abused ears. Its blast shoved me down in my boots. The uproar had scarcely ceased when the pinnace reappeared, dived upon the rear ranks of the foe and let them have a couple there. More disruption. It tied me in knots to see what went up even above the tree-tops.

"Now!" yelled Jay. Grabbing the handicapped Jepson, he tossed him over one shoulder and pounced forward. We drove with him.

Our first obstacle was a huge crater bottomed with tired and steaming earth amid which writhed some mutilated yellow worms. Cutting around the edges of this, I leaped a six-foot length of blasted creeper that, even in death, continued to jerk spasmodically and horribly. Many more odd lengths squirmed between here and the next bomb-hole. All were green inside and out, and bristled with hair-like tendrils that continued to vibrate as if vainly seeking the life that had gone.

The one hundred yards between craters were covered in record time, Jay still in the lead despite his awkward burden. I sweated like a tormented bull and thanked my lucky stars for the low gravity that alone enabled me to maintain this hectic pace.

Again we split our ranks and raced around the ragged rim of the second crater. This brought us practically nose to nose with the enemy and after that all was confusion.

A bush got me. Sheer Terrestrial conditioning made me disregard the darned thing in spite of recent experiences. I had my attention elsewhere and in an instant it had shifted a pace to one side, wrapped itself around my legs and brought me down in full flight. I plunged with a hearty thump, unarmed, but cursing with what little breath I had left. The bush methodically sprinkled my space-suit fabric with a fine grey powder. Then a long, leatherish tentacle snaked from behind me, ripped the bush from my form, tore it to pieces.

"Thanks, Sug Farn," I breathed, got up and charged on.

A second antagonistic growth collapsed before my needler and the potent ray carried straight on another sixty or seventy yards and roasted the guts of a bawling, gesticulating native. Sug side-swiped a third bush, scattered it with scorn. The strange powder it sprayed around did not seem to affect him.

By now Jay was twenty yards ahead. He paused, flung a bomb, dropped, came to his feet and pounded ahead with Jepson still bouncing on one shoulder. The pinnace howled overhead, swooped, created wholesale slaughter in the enemy's rear. A needle-ray spiked from behind me, sizzled dangerously close to my helmet and burned a bush. I could hear in my helmet-phones a constant and monotonous cursing in at least six voices. On my right a great tree lashed around and toppled headlong, but I had neither the time nor inclination to look at it.

Then a snake trapped Blaine. How it had survived in one piece, alone among its torn and tattered fellows, was a mystery. It lay jerking exactly like all the other bits and pieces but still existed in one long lump. Blaine jumped it and at the same instant it curled viciously, wound itself around him. He shrieked into his helmet-microphone. The sound of his dying was terrible to hear. His space-suit sank in where the great coils compressed it and blood spurted out from the folds between. The sight and sound shocked me so much that involuntarily I stopped and Armstrong blundered into me from behind.

"Keep going!" he roared, giving me an urgent shove. With his needler he sliced the green constricter into violently humping sections. We pushed straight on as hard

126

as we could go, perforce leaving Blaine's crushed corpse to the mercy of this alien jungle.

Now we were through the fronting ranks of quasi-vegetable life and into the howling natives whose number had thinned considerably. Brittle globes popped and splintered all around our thudding feet but our suits protected us from the knock-out effects of their gaseous contents. In any case, we were moving too fast to get a deadly whiff. I needled three greenies in rapid succession, saw Jay tear off the head of another without so much as pausing in his weighty onrush.

We were gasping with exertion when unexpectedly the foe gave up. Remaining natives faded with one accord into their protecting forest just as the pinnace made yet another vengeful dive upon them. The way was clear. Not slackening our headlong pace in the slightest, with eyes alert and weapons prepared, we pelted to the waterfront. And there, reposing in the great clearing, we found the sweetest sight in the entire cosmos—the *Marathon*.

It was at this point that Sug Farn put a prime scare into us, for as we sprinted joyfully toward the open airlock, he beat us to it, held up the stump of a tentacle, said, "It would be as well if we do not enter just yet."

"Why not?" demanded Jay. His glowing eyes focused on the Martian's stump, and he added, "What has happened to you?"

"I have been compelled to shed most of a limb," said Sug Farn, mentioning it with the casual air of one to whom shedding a limb is like taking off a hat. "It was that powder. It is composed of a million submicroscopic insects. It crawls around and eats. It started to eat me. Take a look at yourselves."

By hokey, he was right! Now that I came to examine it I could see small patches of grey powder changing shape on the surface of my space-suit. Sooner or later it was going to eat its way through the fabric—and start on me!

I've never felt more thoroughly lousy in my life. So, keeping watch on the nearest fringe of the forest, we had to spend an irritating and sweaty half-hour roasting each other's suits with needlers turned to wide jet and low power. I was well-nigh cooked by the time the last pinhead louse dropped off.

Young Wilson, never the one to pass up a public humiliation, seized the opportunity to dig out a movie camera and record our communal decontamination. I knew that this eventually would be shown to an amused world sitting in armchair comfort far, far from the troubles surrounding Rigel. Secretly I hoped that somehow a quota of surviving bugs would manage to get around to the film and lend a taste of realism to the fun.

With a more official air, Wilson also took shots of the forest, the river, and a couple of upturned alien boats with all their bivalve paddles exposed. Then, thankfully, we piled into the ship.

The pinnace was lugged aboard and the *Marathon* took off without delay. There's never been a time when I felt more like a million dollars than at the moment when normal and glorious yellow-white light poured through the ports and the bilious green colouring departed from our faces. With Brennand standing at my side, I watched this strange, eerie world sink below, and I can't say I was sorry to see it go.

Jay came along the catwalk and informed, "Sergeant, we're making no further landings. The skipper has decided to return to Terra forthwith and make a full report."

"Why?" asked Brennand. He gestured toward the diminishing sphere. "We've come away with practically nothing worth having."

"McNulty thinks we've learned enough to last us for a piece." The rhythmic hum of the stern tubes filled in his brief period of silence. "McNulty says he's conducting an exploratory expedition and not managing a slaughterhouse. He's had enough and is thinking of tendering his resignation."

"The officious dope!" said Brennand, with shameful lack of reverence.

"And *what* have we learned, if anything?" I inquired.

"Well, we know that life on that planet is mostly symbiotic," Jay replied. "It's different forms of life share their existence and their faculties. Men share with trees, each according to his kind. The communal point is that queer chest organ."

"Drugs for blood," said Brennand, showing disgust.

"But," Jay continued, "there are some higher than the Ka, higher than all others, some so high and godlike that they could depart from their trees and travel the globe by day or by night. They could milk their trees, transport the life-giving fluids and absorb them from bowls. Of the symbiotic partnership imposed upon them, they had gained the mastery and—in the estimation of the planet—they alone were free."

"How are the mighty fallen!" I offered.

"Not so," Jay contradicted. "We have fought our way out of their power—but we have not conquered them. The world remains theirs and theirs alone. We are retiring with losses, and we have yet to find a way to cure Jepson."

A thought struck me as he turned to go. "Hey, what happened after that assault on the ship. And how did you keep track of us?"

"It was a losing fight. Discretion became the better part of valour. So we blew free before they could incapacitate the ship. After that, we followed you very easily." His eyes always remained inscrutably aflame but I will swear that a touch of malicious humour came into them as he went on, "You had Sug Farn with you. We had Kli Yang and the rest of his gang." He tapped his head suggestively. "The Martians have much *gamish*."

"They're telepathic among themselves," yelped Brennand, flushing with ire. "I forgot all about that. Sug Farn never said a word. The cross-eyed spider just slept every chance he got."

"Nevertheless," said Jay, "he was in constant touch with his fellows."

He went along the catwalk, rounded the far corner. Then the warning alarm sounded and Brennand and I clung like brothers while the ship switched to Flettner drive. The green world faded to a dot with swiftness that never fails to astound me. Taking fresh hold on ourselves, we rubbed our distorted innards into shape. Then Brennand gripped the valve of the starboard airlock, turned the control, watched the pressure gauge crawl from three pounds up to fifteen.

"The Martians are inside there," I pointed out. "And they won't like it."

"I don't want 'em to like it. I'll teach those rubber caricatures to hold out on us!"

"McNulty won't like it, either!"

"Who cares what McNulty likes or dislikes!" he bawled. Then McNulty himself suddenly came around the corner, walking with portly dignity.

Brennand promptly added in still louder tones, "You ought to be ashamed of yourself, talking like that. You ought to be more respectful and refer to him as the skipper."

Look, if ever you take to the spaceways don't worry too much about the ship—concentrate your worrying on the no-good bums who'll share it with you!

MESMERICA

I had counted on twelve well-earned months amid the soothingly familiar surroundings of Earth, but this was another simple sum that added up wrong. Some infernal nosey-poke in an observatory saw fit to convince the powers-that-be that possible part-dirt existed in the region of Cassiopoeia. Whereupon a fist-full of telegrams went to all the tired and trusted suckers requesting the pleasure of their heart's blood.

Mine came at three o'clock in a warm, mellow afternoon when I was busily occupied rocking on the verandah. Let me tell you that's no sort of time or place in which to view with approval an invitation to throw away one's arms and legs. I felt like telling the bearer off except that it wasn't his fault. So I read it and tore it up and said to heck with it and went on rocking with my eyes closed. Next day I packed and departed east to swallow the bait solely because I lacked the moral courage to refuse it. I hadn't enough guts to be a coward.

So that's why for the umpteenth time I stood by a port moodily watching a new world swell into gigantic view. Despite my lack of enthusiasm the sight became so absorbing that I almost forgot to jump into harness before the *Marathon* played its Flettner trick preparatory to landing. As it was, I made it in the nick of time. Came the usual feeling of being turned inside-out and we were there.

My proper post was in the armoury, and there I stayed while in the main cabin they chose the names of those whose backsides were to be offered for any alien kicks that might be coming. After previous experiences there wasn't quite the same bumptious enthusiasm for hitting the dirt without care, permission, or weapons. Leastways,

131

nobody beat McNulty to the mark by crawling out through the tubes this time.

The nearest observation-port framed a mass of vegetable growths of every imaginable description. They had one uncommon feature that struck me immediately, namely, that nothing was tangled around anything else. Tall or short, slender or wide-spreading, each growth stood in its own appropriate plot of ground and let a thin spray of sunlight reach the earth between its neighbours and itself. A jungle that wasn't a jungle. One could stroll through it without trouble so far as obstacles to one's feet were concerned, though there might well be other and more effective forms of opposition.

Green was the predominant colour with here and there an odd patch of yellow or brown. The chlorophyll reaction seems common to vegetation in most parts of the cosmos where quality of solar radiation favours it. The sun's rays showed golden where they struck through gaps between growths. This world's primary closely resembled Old Sol but was a trifle hotter because a little nearer.

I felt a bit uneasy as I studied the scene outside. This strange live-and-let-live orderliness of plant-life registered with an eerie touch of artificiality. I could distinguish no organised regularity among the growths themselves, no neat patches of one type or tidy rows of another. Nevertheless I had a strong impression that they had been cultivated by some thing or things with ideas radically different from our own. It looked rather as though an alien agriculturalist had mooched around with a sack of widely assorted seeds, setting them at random just as his hand found them, but carefully spacing them according to each one's individual need. Like a man planting an oak twenty feet from a cabbage.

Brennand came along, remarked, "There appears to be a deceitful law governing other worlds, to wit: that they look completely innocent while making ready to bite you."

"You think this one is preparing some mayhem?"

"I don't know. But I'll lay no bets on it being a Garden of Eden."

"Would you bet on it being a garden of some sort?"

"What d'you mean?" He eyed me curiously.

I pointed through the port. "Where's the usual battle for living-space?"

He had a look outside. "That's an easy one. The ground is poor hereabouts. It lacks fertility. So growth is sparse."

"How's that for being sparse?" I inquired, indicating a hairy, cactus-like object half the size of the *Marathon*.

"The stuff grows too haphazardly, anyway," he evaded. "You don't plant a carrot next to a gooseberry bush."

"Somebody else might."

"Why?"

"Oh, heck!" I said, wearily. "Ask a simpler one. Ask me why I'm here when I could be taking it happily and comfortably at home."

"I know the answer to that," he gave back. "There's no morning mail on the *Marathon*."

"So what?"

"Mail contains bills, threatening letters——"

"Hah!" I eyed him carefully. "Judging others by yourself, eh? I've often wondered why you shoot away from Earth like a guy out of a cold bath. So you're being hunted?"

"We are not talking about me," he pointed out. "We are discussing you and your possible motivations. Mine are simple—I like heavy money. These trips provide it."

A nice retort for that one lay ready on my tongue but didn't get voiced. Two engineers named Ambrose and McFarlane arrived at the armoury and demanded their stuff.

"Where are the others?" I inquired, handing out needlers, first-aid packs, emergency rations and so forth.

"There aren't any others."

"Mean to say McNulty is sending out only the pair of you?"

"That's right. Two can handle a lifeboat."

"The old boy is cautious," Brennand commented. "He becomes jumpier every trip."

"You fellows want spacesuits?"

"No." Ambrose nodded toward the port. "It's thirteen pounds and has a faint fragrance of old goat, but it's healthy."

"So that's what I've been smelling all along." I jerked

133

a suitably contemptuous thumb toward Brennand. "I thought it was him."

"You thought it was *he*," said Brennand. "Where's your grammar?"

McFarlane, a thin, wiry, ginger-haired individual, strapped on his needler, flexed his arms, invited, "In case I don't come back does anyone want to kiss me goodbye?" Then he made a face, said, "Oh, well——" and stamped out.

A couple of minutes later the lifeboat blew free, shot westward and hammered into the distance. I could hear the faraway noise of it for quite a time after it had gone from sight.

Mooching along to see Steve Gregory, I found him squatting in his cubby-hole and sucking his teeth.

"Anything doing, Steve?"

He ran a dismal eye over his instruments. "All I get is a sizzle-pop." Then he gestured toward a thick book lying near his right hand. "According to this Radio Koran it is the characteristic discharge of a sun called Zem 27, presumably the one burning outside."

"Nothing else?"

"Nary a thing." Bending forward, he flipped a switch, spoke toward a box. "Speak up, lifeboat—we want to hear from you."

A squeaky voice I couldn't recognise as either Ambrose's or McFarlane's answered, "Forty-four west and eight thousand up."

"See anything?"

"Nothing remarkable."

"Okay. Listening out." He leaned back. "I was under the delusion that my last trip was my last trip. I was all set to take it easy and bake my corns on the stove."

"Same here," I said. "Maybe there's a curse on me. I oughtn't have grabbed that guppy's opal."

"What guppy's opal?" He perked up, raising his eyebrows.

"Never mind. I've a dirty deed contaminating my past."

"Who hasn't?" he retorted. "Back in the good old days on Venus I traded my birth certificate for a——"

Something dinged amid his dials and meters. He flipped a switch.

A voice said a bit louder than before, "Lifeboat here. Seventy west and four thousand up. Circling over a large lake. There's what looks like an encampment on the shore."

"Stand by a moment." Steve worked another switch, said to his mike, "Captain, I've got Ambrose on. He thinks he's found local life."

"Put him through to me," McNulty ordered.

Steve made the connection. We could hear ensuing conversation through the intercom.

"What is it, Ambrose?"

"A camp on the shore of a lake."

"Ah! Who or what is occupying it?"

"Nobody," said Ambrose.

"Nobody? You mean it's deserted?"

"Wouldn't go so far as to say that, but that's how it looks from up here. There are about a hundred small pyramidical huts arranged in four concentric circles. Can't see anything moving around between them." A pause, followed by, "How about us landing and taking a closer look, Captain?"

McNulty didn't like it. The long silence showed him to be mulling it over. Undoubtedly he was trying to think up a way of getting the suggested closer look without going closer to get it. I've never known a man so unwilling to place bets on anything but one hundred per cent certainty. Finally his voice sounded with reduced volume as he spoke in an aside to someone else.

"They want to land. What d'you think of it?"

"Nothing ventured, nothing gained," answered Jay Score's deep tones.

"Yes, I suppose so, but——" Another pause, then he came louder over the intercom. "Look, Ambrose, is there room for the *Marathon* to sit in that place?"

"Not without burning ten acres of bush or flattening half the huts."

"Humph! I'll tell you what: try zooming close over the roofs a couple of times. That ought to bring them out running."

Ambrose sighed and said, "Okay, Captain, we'll try

135

it—but I don't think there's anyone in the place to be brought out." Silence for a long while before he came back with, "No soap."

"They didn't appear?"

"No. We almost brushed the roofs off and our air-blast shook the entire place. It's empty."

"Very well, then. Make your landing and see what you can discover but be mighty careful." His tones drifted away again as he continued, "I tell you, Jay, that after this trip some other commander can———"

Steve cut the switch, said, "He's got the same trouble as you and me. He's hankering for the *Upsydaisy* and the regular Venus-run. We were in a nice comfortable rut there."

"Somebody has to do the heroics," I said.

"I know, I know. But the glory ought to be shared around. It can come one way too often."

He scowled at his instruments and Ambrose's voice came out of them dulled by a steady drumming noise.

"Easy does it, Mac. Watch that row to starboard. Yes, we'll just about make it. Brakes, quick! There!"

The drumming ceased. Then followed a long conversation too much off the mike to hear in ful detail until their voices rose and they started shouting at each other. Seemed they were arguing about which one went out and which stayed with the boat. Seemed that McFarlane wanted to toss for it and Ambrose wanted to examine the coin he proposed to use.

Becoming slightly red in the face, Steve operated a stud that made loud dinging noises and succeeded in attracting the attention of the distant debaters.

"Now see here, you two cretins," he said without courtesy, "each of you pulls a hair from the other's scalp. The one who gets the longest goes out. The short one stays in."

That brought a long silence ended by the sound of an opening and closing airlock.

After a while, Steve snapped impatiently, "Well, who was it?"

"McFarlane," informed Ambrose surily. He went away from his mike, leaving the channel open. For a time we could hear his boots clumping restlessly to and fro within the little boat. Probably he was absorbing an eyeful of the outside through various ports and enviously watching Mc-Farlane strolling around enjoying the country.

After a bit he gave an annoyed grunt, muttered something indistinguishable. His heavy space boots tramped farther away. The airlock opened and we heard his distant voice bawl out of it.

"Well, what d'you want, Bighead?"

The reply from outside couldn't reach the mike, so we didn't know what McFarlane said. There sounded an extremely faint thump as of somebody jumping out the airlock and onto thick grass. Then all went quiet. The minutes crawled by, each one an age.

Steve started to fidget. Later on his eyebrows commenced oscillating. When his large ears also got the jittering jerks it was more than I could stand.

"Look," I said. "Let's not fall to pieces, shall we? Let's say something to Ambrose if it's only to swap limericks."

Giving me the ugly eye he reached for his stud, dinged the far-off receiver a dozen times, listened for a response. Ambrose didn't reply. Neither did McFarlane. The boat remained as silent as the grave though a faint and steady hum showed that its transmitter was still active and holding the channel open.

Taking his mike, Steve hoarsed into it, "Lifeboat! Are you there, lifeboat? We're calling you! Answer us, lifeboat!"

Silence.

"Ambrose!" he howled into the mike. "AMBROSE! *Are you there?*"

No response.

"Maybe he's gone to pay a visit," I suggested uneasily.

"What for?" asked Steve, acting stupid.

"To trim his moustache or something. People pay visits, don't they? That's what the little room is for."

"Not at *this* time," he said.

"What the heck has that got to do with it? He doesn't go by his watch."

"He could pick a better time than this," he persisted. Then he waggled the eyebrows a bit and added, "Anyway, I'll give him another ten minutes."

137

At the end of that period he dinged and bawled and did everything he knew.

The lifeboat gave back its low hum and nothing more.

We had to tell McNulty, of course. He foamed and fumed and discussed it with Jay. They decided it couldn't yet be taken for granted that anything untoward had happened at the other end. Possibly Ambrose's curiosity had overcome his caution and he'd left the boat to look at something his partner had found. Or maybe he'd had to go out to help haul aboard something that needed two men's strength to handle. But he ought to have said so first. He ought to have reported his intentions and the reasons for them before leaving. There would be harsh words about this omission when he returned.

Meanwhile we'd sit tight and listen out. We'd give them at least another hour before taking alarm. So I left Steve to sit and wait, went to the galley and gave myself a meditative meal. Young Wilson was there swilling coffee.

"How's the boat doing?" he inquired.

"That's the current mystery." I bolted a wad, filled a mug of black java.

"Meaning what?"

"Meaning it has squatted in a village and shut up. Steve can't get a squeak out of it."

"A village? What sort of creatures are inhabiting it?"

"No sort. It's empty. So Ambrose and McFarlane have gone in and made it emptier."

"They've disappeared?"

"I wouldn't say that."

"You wouldn't be surprised, either," he suggested, giving me a leery look.

"No, I would not."

"Hey, hey!" He made a face at the wall. "Here we go again." Then he went on, "What's McNulty doing about it?"

"Nothing just yet."

"Heck, those two guys may be cooked and eaten while we hang around resting."

"Or maybe they're cooking and eating something worth having while we're trying to masticate this dog-food." I poked the rest of the wad away, finished the java, got up. "See you in somebody's oven."

Spent most of the next hour busy in the armoury, then let the remainder of the work wait. I was too restless to concentrate on it because I had to know what was going on. So back I went to Steve's place.

"Any——?"

"Sh-h-h!" He held a warning finger to his lips. "Not a sound up to now but it's just started coming through."

He turned up the volume. There came the characteristic crack of an airlock door closing. Then something like the clunk of boots shuffling around at the tail-end of the distant lifeboat. Steve put out a finger, prodded the stud. Back came the loud ding of the faraway receiver's call-bell.

It was followed immediately by a peculiar sound from the opposite end of the boat. A kind of hiss or spit. Gave me the eerie impression of something non-human startled by the ding. The boot sounds didn't repeat. No tramping forward to answer the summons, as we had expected. Just the sharp spit and silence.

Frowning, Steve dinged again. No answer. Yet somebody was in the boat, of that we had no doubt. He dinged half a dozen times in quick succession, making it urgent and ireful. He might as well have been trying to line up three lemons for all the good it did.

"What the blazes has come over them?" he demanded.

"Try some bad language," I offered. "That loudspeaker of theirs can be heard from nose to tail."

Taking the mike, he bellowed, *"Hey!"*

The response to that was a louder hiss like a railroad locomotive letting go a quirt of surplus steam, also a swift clatter of bootlike noises followed by the crash of the airlock door. Then nothing. Whatever had been in the boat had gone out, and hurriedly.

Steve gaped at me, his face a mixture of emotions. "What d'you think of that?"

"I don't like it."

"Neither do I." He stared doubtfully at his microphone. "Do you suppose they're acting up because they don't want to be ordered back just yet?"

"Could be," I admitted. "Nothing of which the human

mind can conceive is impossible. So by a million to one chance they may have stumbled across a cosmic cocktail bar run by a pair of voluptuous brunettes. But I don't think so. That radio talks trouble to me."

"Me, too. I'm going to tell McNulty." Changing intercom lines, he got the captain, said, "Somebody's just been in that lifeboat and wouldn't answer."

"You're sure of that?"

"Positive, Captain. I could hear the movements as plain as the nose on my face."

"You couldn't put it more convincingly," said McNulty. "It wasn't Ambrose or McFarlane?"

Steve hesitated, said, "If it was, they've gone deaf on us. They won't respond to the call-bell. And when I yelled, 'Hey!' they beat it."

"This is ominous," decided McNulty. "We had better move fast and——" He ceased as the loudspeaker in our little cubby-hole suddenly squawked, "Hey!" Then he said in startled tones, "What was *that?*"

"The lifeboat." With his ears trying to go fourteen ways at once, Steve juggled with switches. "I'll put it through to you."

"Now look here, Ambrose," began McNulty, authoritatively pompous. "What's the game?"

"Now look here, Ambrose," sneered the lifeboat in peculiarly stitlted tones. "What's the game?"

"This is Captain McNulty talking!" roared that worthy, his blood pressure beginning to rise.

"This is Captain McNulty talking," squealed the lifeboat in outrageous imitation.

McNulty breathed heavily, then inquired in a low, almost unbearable voice, "Steve, are you playing tricks with me?"

"No, sir," said Steve, shocked at the notion.

The other bellowed afresh. "Ambrose, I order you to return forthwith and by hokey——!" He broke off. There was a pause while the lifeboat repeated this in high-pitched and penetrating mockery. Then a new voice took his place.

"Who's there?" asked Jay Score, calmly and self-possessed.

"Who's there?" inquired the lifeboat.

140

"Yimmish vank wozzeneck," said Jay in sheer nonsense.

"Yimmish vank wozzeneck," echoed the lifeboat, as though one language were equally as good as another.

Jay said decisively, "Close the line, Steve. We'll send out the pinnace to look into this."

Steve closed the line, said to me, "I think Ambrose has bought himself a parrot."

"Or a cut throat." I slid a finger across my gullet, made a gurgling sound.

He didn't like it.

Eight of us went in the pinnace, all Terrestrials. A couple of the Martians were reluctantly willing to leave their chessboards but there was no reason to suppose we'd need their help and they'd take up too much room in the boat. Jay Score didn't join the party either, which was a pity in view of the peculiar circumstances. He'd have been useful in ways we had yet to realise.

Bannister did the piloting. The pinnace boomed away from the *Marathon's* side, went up to ten thousand feet. Clouds spread thin and high on this world, so that visibility remained pretty good in all directions. Looking through the port beside my seat I could see sparsely wooded landscape stretching for miles, with rivers and streams here and there and long, rolling hills in the distance. There didn't seem to be any outstanding evidence of intelligent life, leastways, not around these parts.

Sitting next to me, young Wilson nursed a camera that was smothered with gadgets and had a greenish filter over its lens. He kept staring out the port on his side, then at the sun, and licking his lips. In front, alongside Bannister, a blue-jowled character named Veitch was talking to Steve through a larynx-mike.

The pinnace hammered on for quite a while before it went into a wide starboard turn and lost height. Bannister and Veitch leaned forward scanning the lay of the land through their windshield. Soon we could see the cleared patch by the river, the concentric circles of huts and the lifeboat lying nearby. We went lower, still turning. It became evident that there wouldn't be room to land without bashing up something; the grounded lifeboat fitted neatly into the only available space.

Perforce we droned beyond clear sight of this layout, being unable to turn in a circle small enough to keep going round its edge. We lost a lot more height, came back, crossed the camp at no more than five hundred feet, saw Ambrose and McFarlane lounging by the boat and staring up at us. I could hardly believe it, they looked so casual. We flashed past them in about two seconds, with Wilson snapping his camera at them through the port.

I hadn't got a very good view of the pair on the ground, what with Wilson confiscating most of the seeing space, but I gained the impression that both were unharmed and perfectly at ease. Also that Ambrose was nursing something that looked like a basket of fruit. It annoyed me more than somewhat. I had the notion that the pair of them had wandered around pandering to their guts while panic hit the *Marathon* and brought the pinnace out. Fat lot they cared so long as they could stuff their bellies. But they'd pay for it: McNulty would skin them alive in due time.

We made another U-turn, came over in a second run. Bannister made menacing gestures at them from behind the windshield. McFarlane waved back airily, as though he were on a Sunday school outing. Wilson snapped him doing it.

Veitch was saying into his mike, "They're all right. The lifeboat must have developed a radio fault to account for the stuff you heard."

I don't know what the *Marathon* answered to that, but Veitch finished, "All right. We'll drop them a note and come straight back."

He scribbled on paper, attached it to a weighted message-streamer and slung it through the base-trap at the next run over. I saw its long ribbon go fluttering down twenty yards from the pair of beachcombers below. Then we thrummed beyond view and headed back to the mother ship.

Was on my way to the armoury when Steve spotted me from his cubby-hole and called me in. He surveyed me as if trying to decide whether I were drunk or sober.

After a bit, he said, "You sure those two bums are okay?"

"I saw them with my own eyes. Why?"

"Well . . . well——" He swallowed, gloomed at his meters and switches, shifted back to me. "Their boat *could* develop a fault. Nothing is perfect and that goes for radio apparatus as much as anything else."

"So what?"

"I've never heard of a defect that causes messages to be bounced back word for word as spoken."

"You have now!" I said. "There's always a first time."

"It's contrary to theory," he insisted.

"So's my Aunt Martha. She has ten toes."

"Everybody has," he said.

"Yes, but not two on one foot and eight on the other."

He scowled slightly and maintained, "I'm not interested in circus freaks. I'm telling you there can be no such thing as a fault producing echo-symptoms."

"Then how d'you explain it?"

"I can't." He let go a deep sigh. "That's just it. I heard what I heard and there's nothing wrong with my ears and it wasn't a radio fault. I tell you, somebody was giving us the yah-boo and I don't think it funny."

"Ambrose wouldn't be so childish," I said.

"No, he wouldn't," he agreed meaningfully.

"McFarlane is no juvenile delinquent, either."

"No, he isn't," he said in the same way.

"Then who else?"

"Oh, shut up—I don't believe in poltergeists."

With that I continued on my way, feeling rather unsettled but refusing to show it. Steve knew his stuff all right. None better. He was the boat's radio expert. And he was so certain of himself about this matter.

So somebody had slung McNulty's words back in his teeth. It wasn't Ambrose. It wasn't McFarlane. It couldn't be anyone else. Yet none of us had imagined it. The more one thought of this phenomenon the more inexplicable it became. Yet nothing is completely inexplicable so far as alien planets are concerned.

Reassured by the pinnace's report, McNulty relaxed sufficiently to let a few men exercise their legs outside. No more than a dozen, with strict orders to retain their needlers ready to hand and not to go more than half a mile from the ship. The lucky dozen were picked from a hat and did not include yours truly.

They came for their weapons. One of them was Jepson, the guy who'd gotten himself all gummed up last trip.

I cracked, "What are you letting yourself in for this time?"

"Nothing if I can help it," he assured with some fervour.

Molders, the big Swede, took a projector, remarked, "I'm keeping my distance from you, anyway. I've had enough of sticking together."

They went out. The sky showed they wouldn't have long to ramble around because the sun already was low and there wasn't much more than another hour to nightfall.

The first shades had drawn long and dark when McNulty got the willies again. Half a dozen of the liberty boys had returned of their own accord, having found nothing outside to detain them. The ship's siren sounded with a horrid moan, recalling the others. There was some excitement up at the bow end and I noticed the pom-pom crew checking one of their multi-barrelled weapons. Something was brewing sure enough and Steve was the man likeliest to know the cause. I went to see him.

"What's up now?"

"The pinnace dropped a message to the lifeboat, didn't it?" he said.

"It did. I watched it go down."

"Well, they've taken no notice of it." He jerked a thumb at the nightshrouded observation port on his left. "It's gone sundown and they're still sitting tight. Neither are they responding to my radio calls. I've dinged until I'm sick of it. I've bawled at them until I'm hoarse. The lifeboat's generator is still running and the channel remains open, but Ambrose and McFarlane might be the other side of the cosmos for all I can tell."

"Can't understand it." I was frankly puzzled. "I saw them myself, taking it easy outside their airlock. Nothing wrong with either of them. And the boat itself was undamaged."

"I don't care," he asserted stubbornly. "I told you before that there's something mighty fishy about this and I say so again."

There wasn't anything useful I could add, so I mooched off, lay in my bunk and tried to read but found I couldn't concentrate no matter how I tried. The feeling that we'd had a fast one pulled on us in some mysterious way grew stronger and stronger, I became jumpier the more I thought about it but for the life of me couldn't conjure up a satisfactory explanation.

Outside, darkness now was complete save for light from the stars faintly illuminating surrounding vegetation. I was still stewing the problem of the apparently mutinous pair with the lifeboat, trying to decide what could keep them there despite all orders to the contrary, when a knock sounded on the door of my cabin and Wilson came in.

The look on his face made me sit up quick. He had the appearance of one who has unwittingly shaken hands with a ghost.

"What's eating you?" I demanded. "Got the colly-wobbles or something? If so, don't you be sick over me!"

"I don't know what I've got." He sat on the edge of the desk, tried to compose himself but didn't succeed very well. "I'm on my way to see McNulty about it. But first I'd like you to check up and assure me that I'm not nuts."

"Check up? on what?"

"On these." He tossed three half-plate photographs into my lap.

I gave them a cursory glance, noted that they were the pics he'd taken from the pinnace. Considering the awkward circumstances in which they'd been made they'd turned out pretty good. He must have snapped at one-thousandth of a second or even less, and with his lens open wider than a Venusian guppy's mouth. No blurs attributable to the pinnace's fast motion. Sharp and clear as though taken from a standstill.

"Nice work," I complimented. "You certainly know how to handle a camera."

He stared at me with a slight touch of incredulity, then said, "How about taking a closer look. See if you can find the zipper on Ambrose's hug-me-tight."

Obediently I took a closer look. Then I shot headlong out of the bunk, switched on my powerful desk-light and had another gander beneath its revealing brilliance. I went all wishy-washy. A long, thin icicle substituted itself for my spine.

There wasn't any Ambrose.

There wasn't any McFarlane.

Precisely where they had stood outside the lifeboat's airlock were two repulsive objects resembling tangled masses of thick, black, greasy rope.

"Well?" inquired Wilson, watching me.

I shoved the pics into his hands. "You'd better take these to bow cabin at the double. I'm going to lay out the needlers and stuff—they'll be wanted before long!"

The general alarm sounded ten minutes later. I was expecting it and went forward on the run. We gathered in the main cabin, silent and full of anticipation. McNulty strutted in with Jay Score following right behind, huge and shiny-eyed.

McNulty said with a trace of bitterness, "We have made contact with this planet's highest life-form some hours ago but not realised it until now. They're hostile and they've gained the edge of us. The first loss is ours. We're already down by four men.'"

"Four?" I ejaculated involuntarily.

His eyes strayed to me a moment, went back over the others. "I permitted twelve to go out. Only ten have returned. Jepson and Painter have not answered the recall siren. Neither do Ambrose and McFarlane respond to my orders to return. It leaves me no choice but to regard those four as probable casualties." His voice hardened. "We must suffer no more!"

The men fidgeted a bit. By my side Kli Yang leaned to whisper to me and Brennand.

"He is counting the pieces without detailing the moves. How can one analyse the trend of the game with insufficient——?"

He shut up as McNulty continued. "The true nature of the opposition is not yet fully understood but it is evident that they have mesmeric power not to be despised. Doubtless they used it to entice Ambrose from the lifeboat, making him think he was being summoned by McFarlane. That will give you some idea of what we're up against."

Brennand, who didn't know the half of what had been

going on, asked, "What d'you mean by mesmeric power, Captain?"

"In the fullest sense that is something we have yet to discover," responded McNulty, making it sound ominous. "All we do know is that they can delude you into thinking you see what they want you to see—and maybe they can take it farther than that! We're facing a mental weapon of considerable potency and we've got to watch our step!"

"Does that apply to Jay?" inquired Brennand. "Can *he* be kidded too?"

It was a good question. Those brilliant eyes didn't function organically like ours. Their optic nerves were thin veins of silver and the brain behind was electronically unique. Wilson's camera hadn't been fooled and for the same reasons I couldn't see how Jay could be, either.

But Jay merely smiled and said, "I have yet to face a test."

Kli Yang chipped in with irritating superiority. "That also applies to us Martians." He made his saucer eyes look two ways at once, pointing them at almost opposite extremes. It gave me the heebies to watch him do it. "As is evident, our optics are superior to Terrestrial organs."

"Nuts!" said Brennand.

"It doesn't matter what sort of eyes you've got so long as the brain can be deceived," Jay Score pointed out.

"That won't be so easy either," declared Kli Yang. He waggled a tentacle by way of emphasis. "Because as is well known, the Martian mind——"

Waving him down in mid-sentence, McNulty said sharply, "This is no time to argue the respective merits of different forms. We're taking action to determine the fate of the missing men and rescue them if still alive. The *Marathon* will remain here while a search-party under Jay Score hunts for Jepson and Painter. At the same time ten men and one Martian will take the pinnace to the lifeboat, burn down an adequate landing-space nearby and look for Ambrose and McFarlane. I want volunteers for both parties."

Ten men and one Martian would overload the pinnace with a vengeance. But the boat hadn't far to go and it certainly was the quickest way to get a rescue party there the stronger in number, the better. I guessed the Martian had been included despite his greater weight because McNulty hoped there might be something in Kli Yang's claim to see straight when he was most cockeyed. The *Marathon's* party was being put under Jay Score for a similar reason: that they'd have the benefit of a leader who couldn't be deluded.

I volunteered to go with the pinnace. So did Bannister, Brennand, Kli Yang, Molders, Wilson, Kelly and several others. Sending the rest of the crew back to their posts until he was ready to organise their outing, McNulty dealt with us first.

"Six men and one Martian will conduct the search," he ordered. "You will keep close together at all times and not permit yourselves to be separated even for a moment. The remaining four will stay in the pinnace and not leave it in any circumstances whatsoever." He stared hard at us, added firmly, "I want that to be thoroughly understood. The four in the boat do not leave the vessel even if the search-party reappears and begs on bended knees for them to come out—because by that time the search-party may not be what it looks to be!"

"Suppose they don't beg us to come out?" asked the lavishly tattooed Kelly. I noticed that he was dangling an outsized spanner from one fist.

McNulty saw the tool at the same time, remarked acidly, "You can leave that object behind. A needler will be more useful." He sniffed his disdain and continued, "It will be all right, of course, if they don't try to tempt you to emerge. The problem then doesn't arise."

"So we let them in?" said Kelly, pointedly.

Hah! The skipper's face was a picture worth seeing. He opened his mouth, shut it, went pink and then red. He turned to Jay Score, making tangled motions with his hands.

"He's raised an issue there, Jay. If the party has been long out of sight, how are those in the pinnace to know whether it's safe to admit them?"

Jay thought it over. "The simplest solution is to use passwords, a different one for each man. The one who can't or won't give it gets needled on the spot. That'll be tough on anyone with a lousy memory but we can't afford to take chances."

148

The skipper didn't care overmuch for the idea and neither did we. Something more positive, more watertight would have been better. If these alien creatures could fool us visually it was remotely possible that they could also kid us audibly, making us imagine that they were saying the right words at the right moment. I had an unpleasant feeling that they might be able to persuade us to draw up a last will and testament in their favour, in the dumb belief that they were our natural heirs.

However, none of us could think up anything better on the spur of the moment. Blood tests would have been an ideal solution, but you can't take samples and subject them to microscopic examination in circumstances where the people being tested may be trying to get aboard six jumps ahead of a pursuing army. A man could die helplessly and messily while we were trying to prove beyond doubt that he was a man!

Leaving McNulty to summon and get on with his briefing of the *Marathon's* own search-party, we hastened with the task of stripping the pinnace of all surplus weight and replacing it with other things more likely to be needed. Being a sort of triple-sized lifeboat, the pinnace normally carried bulky items that wouldn't be wanted on a local trip, such as a ton of emergency rations, enough water to last its crew for two months, oxygen flasks, spacesuits, a cosmic compass, a long-range beam radio and so forth. Dragging all that out, we installed a pom-pom and extra ammo, a gas projector, a case of bombs and a few other unfriendly gifts to natives.

I was staggering past the port airlock with a couple of pom-pom ammo belts draped around me when I noticed that one of the grease monkeys on duty there had operated the door-wind and the plug was rotating inward along its worm. The other grease monkey leaned against the facing wall, picking his teeth and watching the plug glassy-eyed. Both of them had the casual air of stevedores about to preside over the loading of twenty sacks of Venusian marshpods.

Generally I mind my own business because it's the only way to get along when a bunch of you are confined in a bottle and likely to tread on each other's necks if not

149

careful. Perhaps recent events had made me touchy, because this time I stopped dead with the ammo clattering around me.

"Who ordered you to open up?"

"Nobody," informed the tooth picker. "Painter's come back and he wants in."

"How d'you know that?"

"Because we can see him standing outside." He gave me one of those what's-it-got-to-do-with-you looks and added, "He banged on the door. Maybe something's happened to Jepson and he's come to get help."

"Maybe," I said, shucking off the ammo belts and groping for my needler. "And maybe not!"

The door reached the end of its worm while he gaped at me as if I'd taken leave of my senses. It swung aside, revealing a great hole in the dark. Painter clambered into the hole as though a thousand devils were after him and started walking along the cut-out in the worm.

I said loudly, "Stand where you are!"

He did not take the slightest notice. Neither did he answer. He knew me well enough to come back with "What the heck's eating you, Sergeant?" or something like that, and if he had done it he'd have got away with it. But he didn't say a word.

For a split second I watched him, unable to credit the evidence of my own eyes, because I could actually *see* that he was Painter from the hobnails on his boots to the widow's peak in his black hair. He was accurate in every detail, clothes and all. So utterly perfect that I had a horrible fear I was about to commit a cold-blooded murder.

I needled him. The ray caught him square in the guts before he'd come a yard inward.

What happened then stirred my back hairs and made the pair of onlookers feel sick. Something seemed to go click back of my eyes, the vision of Painter disappeared as though cut off from a suddenly extinguished epidiascope. In its place was a violently squirming mass of black rope that tried to tie itself into a million knots. Ends and loops stuck out of the tangle, throbbing and vibrating. There weren't any eyes, nose, ears, or other recognisable organs; nothing but a ball of greasy coils like a dozen

150

pythons knotted in one agonized lump. It rolled backward, fell out just as my ray spiked it again.

"Quick!" I bawled, a trickle of sweat running down my back. "Shut that door!"

They did it sluggishly, like men in a dream. One lugged the lever, the door swung across began to wind into its worm. I stayed there until it had gone all the way and rotation had ceased. There was a faint smell in the air-lock, making me think of the time some guppies had roasted a goat without taking the hide off.

Jay Score came along as I was dragging the ammo belts off the floor and heaving them onto my shoulders. He sampled the air, had a look at the self-conscious grease monkeys and knew without being told that there had been dirty work at the crossroads.

"What's been going on?" he demanded.

"Painter came back," I informed. "Only it wasn't Painter."

"You let him in?"

"Yes. And he was Painter beyond all argument. I knew him better than I know my own mother."

"And so——?"

"But he wouldn't or couldn't talk. He wouldn't answer back. So I took a chance." I thought of it and felt another bead of sweat going down between my shoulder blades. "I rayed him amidships and he turned into something out of a nightmare."

"H'm! Pity I wasn't here myself—it would have pro-vided an opportunity to check on whether I see the same as you see." He thought awhile, went on, "By the looks of it they aren't capable of speech nor of deluding us that they can speak. That simplifies matters a little. Ought to make things easier."

"They were easier on the Venus-run," I remarked with unashamed nostalgia.

Taking no notice, he went on, "We also know that they've actually got Painter and probably Jepson as well, else they wouldn't be able to put over a plausible picture of one of them." He turned to the pair on duty in the lock. "Don't open that door again without first getting permis-sion from the skipper. That's an order!"

They nodded glumly. Jay continued on his way and I

went mine. The pinnace was ready within the hour. We piled in, a tight-fitting little mob with no room to dance around. Kli Yang sat with his head-and-shoulder piece exhausted to three pounds pressure, his long, rubbery tentacles sprawling across half a dozen laps. One of his tips rested on my knees, half turned to expose a sucker the size of a small saucer. I had a crazy desire to spit in it for no other reason than because it was sure to annoy him.

The pinnace boomed away into the dark, Bannister piloting as before. Despite intense gloom of night it wasn't difficult to steer a direct course to the lifeboat. We had a powerful searchight in the bow, a full quota of blind-flying instruments. What helped most was the fact that the lifeboat's generators continued to function and its radio channel remained open: all we had to do was pick up the background noise and follow it to its source.

Pretty soon we roared across the alien encampment with our beam making the grounded lifeboat shine like a silver cylinder at one side. The glimpse we got of the collection of pyramidical huts was extremely brief, but I fancied I saw a few dark, shapeless things moving about the camp. Couldn't be sure of it, thought.

Bannister let go a string of tiny jelly-bombs just as we cleared the camp. They flopped in a straight line covering four or five hundred yards, burst into fierce, all-consuming flame. We thundered onward, giving the blaze time to work itself out, then made a wide circle that took us over some hills, back across the lake. Finally we topped the huts at a height of fifty feet, shaking every roof in the place, and belly-slid to a landing along the ashy path cleared by the bombs.

Four were picked to stay with the boat and hold it against all comers—which included those going out if they happened to be forgetful! The stayers made careful note of our passwords. Mine was *nanifani,* which is a rude word on Venus. Being just an ordinary space-sailor, and no intellectual, I learn all the rude words first and remember them longest. But I never thought the day would come when vulgarity would be a survival-factor.

Those preliminaries over, we checked needlers, pocketed a bomb apiece. Brennand opened the airlock, went

152

out, followed by Molders, Kelly, myself, then Kli Yang and Wilson, in that order. I remember staring at the dancing girl tattooed on Kelly's arm as he made his jump to the ground. He had parted from his inevitable spanner and had a needler in his fist for a change. Then I jumped down and the over-eager Kli Yang landed on top of me, rolling me around in a mess of tentacles. Somehow I wriggled out from under him, making suitable remarks about the Red Planet's facility for producing imbeciles.

Darkness was stygian. One could barely discern the skeletal shapes of unharmed trees and bushes beyond the areas of ash. We had powerful hand-beams but didn't use them lest they make us targets of unknown weapons. When you're up against a strange enemy you have to use a modicum of caution, even if it means feeling around like a blind man.

But we knew where the encampment lay with reference to the pinnace, and all we needed to do was follow the ash-track back to its beginning. The first and most logical place to seek Ambrose and McFarlane—or their bodies—was among those huts. So we made toward them, moving quietly and warily, in single file.

Trouble started at the end of the ash-track and within twenty jumps of the camp. Before us stood a patch of bushes and trees over which the first jelly-bomb had skipped, and beyond those were some of the outer ring of huts faintly visible in the starlight. I don't think we could have recognized the queer shapes as huts had we not been expecting them and been plodding through the gloom long enough for our eyes to get adjusted.

Brennand stepped cautiously through the first of the trees with Molders a couple of yards behind. Next instant there was a dull *thunk!* and a startled exclamation from Molders. The big Swede paused a second or two, his eyes seeking Brennand who seemed to have vanished. Then he took a few tentative steps forward, peering into the blackness, and we heard a second *thunk!*

The third in line was Kelly, who stopped and whispered hoarsely, "There's something indecent around here. I'm going to show a light."

We crowded up to him as he aimed his hand-beam straight ahead. Its circle of brilliant illumination revealed Brennand and Molders sprawling in the undergrowth like kids gone to sleep in the hay. There was nothing whatever to indicate what had conked them, no sign of alien life, no surreptitious sounds in the dark. For all one could tell they'd both decided to drop dead. But even as we looked, Molders sat up, tenderly felt the back of his turnip, his expression stupefied. Brennand twitched a couple of times and let go a bubbling noise.

Blinking into the strong light, Molders complained, "I got slugged!" He struggled upright, stared around, became filled with sudden fury and exclaimed, "I think it was that tree!"

So saying, he needled a five-foot growth standing alongside. I thought he'd gone crazy. Next instant I wondered whether I'd become a bit cracked myself.

The tree posed there, a nondescript object with long, thin, glossy leaves; manifestly and beyond all doubt a genuine one hundred per cent vegetable. Molders' needle-ray hit it squarely in the trunk and at once it disappeared like a fragmentary dream. In its place was one of those horribly knotted balls I'd seen before.

Right behind the irate Molders stood another, similar growth. Despite the intensity of my concentration upon what was happening, one corner of my eye saw this second object quiver as if about to do something. I don't think I've ever pulled a needler faster. I had it out and flaring in less time than it takes to sniff. And that tree also flashed into a greasy black sphere of madly writhing rope.

I kept the needler going and Molders did likewise. There were two features of these squirming bunches of outlandish life that gave me the willies. Firstly, they took the rays in utter silence, without so much as a yelp. Secondly, I sliced off loose ends and projecting loops, whereupon the main body continued to wriggle as though unconscious of its loss while the severed bits jumped and twisted hither and thither with an eerily independent lift of their own.

Well, we sliced them up into a couple of hundred pieces that continued to hump around like sections of giant black worm. Nothing chipped in to stop us and other treelike things nearby stood impassive, unmoving. Maybe they were real trees. Of that, I'll never be sure.

By the time we'd finished, Brennand was on his feet and delicately fingering an egg on his cranium. He took a poor view of the situation, was inclined to be liverish about it.

Giving Kli Yang the sour eye, he said, "You saw those things." He motioned at the squirming pieces. "How did they look to you?"

"I regret to say that they resembled trees," admitted Kli Yang, resenting being duped along with mere Terrestrials.

"Shows the functional superiority of swivel-eyes, doesn't it?" commented Brennand, acidly. He felt his head again, kicked aside a six-inch length of writhing rope. "Come on!"

For some reason or other we broke into a run, reached the first hut and crowded into it together. The edifice proved a lot bigger than it looked from the air: about three times the size of an average room in an Earth-house. It wasn't subdivided but it was furnished according to somebody's outlandish ideas.

The walls and roof were made of reeds woven in complicated patterns so close that they were reasonably windproof and watertight, the whole being mounted on a frame of tough, resilient poles resembling bamboo. The floor was completely covered by a thick grass mat also woven in a theme of repeated curlicues. At one side stood three circular tables a foot high by four in diameter. I call them tables but they might have been chairs or beds for all I know.

A number of peculiar utensils hung from the roof's crosspoles, some of them carved out of solid wood, others of dull, lead-coloured metal. Most of these had thin, curved spouts pierced with a fine hole about large enough to be stoppered with an ordinary pin. Seemed to me that the creature who used these things would suck at them with a mouth as small as a vest button.

What drew our united attention as Brennand's beam focused upon it was an instrument on the wall opposite the door. It had a circular dial marked around the edge with forty-two dots. Another disc bearing one dot on its rim was mounted over this, and while we watched it shifted with almost imperceptible slowness, gradually aligning its own dot against the one on the outer circle. Obviously some kind of clock, though we could not hear it ticking or detect any sound from it at all. However, it served to prove one thing: that we were up against things higher than mere savages, things with a certain amount of cerebral ingenuity and manual dexterity.

Nobody occupied this hut. It stood devoid of inhabitants while its alien clock silently measured alien hours upon the wall. Our beams went over the whole place, not missing a corner, and manifestly it was deserted. At that moment I'd have taken my most binding oath that the hut was vacant, completely vacant—though I did notice a faint goatish smell which I attributed to the stale atmosphere or maybe the effluvia of the late tenants.

Hut number two proved the same. Empty of aliens. It held a bit more furniture differently arranged and had five of the circular tables or beds. Also two clocks. But no owners. We gave it a thorough once-over with six pairs of eyes including Kli Yang's independently swivelling optics, and there wasn't a living thing in evidence.

By the time we'd completed our search of the outer circle by examining hut number thirty, it appeared certain that the encampment's occupants must have beaten it into the bush when first the pinnace roared over, but had left a couple of guards to test our capabilities. Well, we'd shown them a thing or two.

All the same, I didn't feel any too happy about this unopposed stroll around somebody else's home town. Creatures who could make metal utensils and clocklike instruments ought to be able to construct weapons a good deal more formidable than bows and arrows. And that meant that perhaps we'd yet to get a taste of what they had to offer.

Why the delay in kicking our pants? Thinking it over, I realised that one could pick haphazardly on umpteen Terrestrial villages that didn't hold a soldier or a gun. When troops are needed they're summoned by telephone or radio. Maybe we had landed on a bunch of comparative hicks who'd run for help from someplace else. In that event, the fun had yet to come.

I was wrong there. We were having our hair pulled and didn't know it.

Exiting moodily from the thirtieth hut, Brennand said, "I reckon we're wasting our time here."

"You took the words out of my mouth," endorsed Wilson.

"Just what I was thinking," added Molders.

"Me, too," agreed Kelly.

I didn't put in my spoke. It wasn't necessary, with them voicing my own sentiments. I stepped out of the hut and into the dark convinced that all this fiddling around was futile, that it would be best to return to the pinnace and take it away.

"What about the lifeboat?" asked Kli Yang.

"Let it lay," said Brennand, indifferently.

"Well, what about Ambrose and McFarlane?" persisted the Martian, his goggle eyes staring at two of them simultaneously.

"Two needles in a planet-sized haystack," declared Brennand. "We could fumble around for them until we'd got white beards a yard long. Let's go back."

Kli Yang said, "Then what'll we tell McNulty?"

"That we can't find them because they aren't here."

"We don't *know* that."

"I do!" asserted Brennand, peculiarly positive.

"Do you?" There was a pause while Kli Yang stewed this over. Then he asked the others, "Do you feel the same way?"

We all nodded. Yes, me with them—like the dope I am.

"That's strange," observed Kli slowly and with emphasis. "Because *I* don't!"

"So what?" said Kelly, toughly.

Kli Yang turned to him. "My mind is different from yours. My eyes can be fooled—but not something else!"

"What else?"

"Whatever part of my mind is non-visual."

Brennand chipped in with, "Look, what are you trying to say?"

Holding his needler ready in one tentacle-tip and a hand-beam in another, Kli glanced warily around and said, "We came solely to find Ambrose and McFarlane, if they can be found. Now all of a sudden you say the heck with it. You are of one accord." His eyes again tried to probe the night. "Remarkable coincidence, is it not? I think the desire to throw up the search is being imposed upon you—*and that means somebody's here!*"

Boy, it gave me a major jolt! For a couple of heartbeats my mind went into a confused whirl as it tried to cope with two violently opposing concepts. I couldn't see the others' faces more than dimly, but Wilson stood near enough to give me a picture of a man in a mental tangle. Further search was useless: I knew that as surely as I knew I'd got boots on my feet. We were being kidded that further search was useless: I knew that too, with equal certainty.

Then came a kind of snap in my brain as fact triumphed over fancy. It must have happened to the rest at precisely the same moment because Molders let out a loud short of self-disgust, Kelly voiced a hearty curse and Brennand spoke in irritated tones.

"We'll rake through every hut in this place!"

So without further delay we started on the next inner circle. It would have been a good deal quicker if we had dealt with a hut apiece, thus inspecting them six at a time, but we had strict orders to stick together and were beginning to learn sense. A couple of times I found myself on the point of suggesting that we speed up the business by splitting, but on each occasion I bit the words back because the notion might not be truly my own. If I could help it I wasn't taking orders from ropey monstrosities lurking nearby in the dark.

We reached the twelfth hut of this inner row and Brennand went in first, his hand-beam shining ahead of him. By this time we were well-nigh conditioned to expect nobody inside but still held ourselves ready to be proved wrong. Somehow I'd become last in the patrol. I was about to follow Wilson into the hut when from the deep gloom on my right there came a faint sound. I stopped at the door, aimed my beam rightward.

It revealed Ambrose outside the third hut farther along. He waved at my light though it must have been impossible for him to see who was holding it. He didn't seem mussed up in any way and posed there for all the world as if he'd married the daughter of a chief and decided to go native.

Of course I let out a yelp of excitement and called to those in the hut, "One of them is out here."

They poured through the door, got an eyeful of what my beam was showing.

"Hi, Ammy!" called Brennand, starting forward.

"Hi!" said Ambrose, clearly and distinctly, then turned and went into his hut.

Needless to say we went to that edifice at the double, meanwhile wondering whether Ambrose had his hands full with a sick or badly injured McFarlane. It looked like it, the way he'd gone inside instead of coming to join us. I was so sure of finding McFarlane laid out on the floor that instinctively I felt for my first-aid pack. Reaching the hut, we went in. Our six hand-beams flooded the place with light.

And nobody was there.

Nobody!

The walls were firm and tight, devoid of any other exit. Brennand's beam had been steadily focussed on the only door from the moment we started toward it. We went over the inside pretty thoroughly, yelling for Ambrose at intervals, and couldn't find room to hide a rat.

We stood there beaten, and feeling more than liverish, when Molders became smitten with a brainwave. "Why were we lured into *this* hut? Answer: to make us skip the last two!"

"Of course!" breathed Brennand, startled. He jumped for the door. "Never mind orders: we'll divide into threes and take both together."

Molders, Kelly, and I charged expectantly into hut number thirteen. Empty. Furnished more or less similarly to all the others but with nobody in occupation. The other two didn't waste time. Satisfied that they had picked the wrong dump, they chased out to join Brennand's gang next door and I was about to follow when I heard or thought I heard a choking sound behind me.

Turning in the doorway, I lit up the interior, couldn't see anything that might have caused the noise. But even as I looked, it came again, followed by a series of dull,

159

muted thumps as of something beating upon the thick grass carpet.

More illusions, I thought. Though they were normally silent I knew that at least a few of the more talented aliens could make us hear things. I could have sworn Ambrose had said "Hi!" when he'd replied to Brennand. Then it struck me that there *must* be ropey things clever enough to imitate real speech because somebody had parroted McNulty over the radio and that had been no delusion. It had been an actual voice.

Stupidly I called, "Who's there?" and made ready to needle whatever part of the hut jeeringly echoed, "Who's there?" No voice came back but the choking and thumping sounds responded with greater vigour.

My mind argued with itself. "You've allowed yourself to become separated from the others even if only by a few yards. They're all in the next hut, unable to see what happens to you—and something wants you to go to that corner and get bopped."

Curiosity pulled me one way, caution the other. And just then Kelly returned to see what was keeping me. That settled the matter.

"Half a second," I said. "You stand by and cover me—there's something funny here."

With that I went into the hut, beam in one hand, needler in the other, traced the noises to the farther left-hand corner. They got loud as I neared, as if to tell me I was warm in this daffy game of blind man's buff. Now I could hear them almost as clearly as the *Marathon's* bellow when she goes over to boost-point. Feeling more than silly in front of the onlooking Kelly, I dumped the beam on the floor, knelt beside it, felt around and put my hand on a heavy boot.

The next instant Kelly rapped out a vulgar word and squirted his needle-ray about three inches over the back of my neck. The heat of it scorched the hairs just above my collar. Something moved closely and violently behind me, a couple of metal utensils clattered as they got thrown across the room, and a four-inch section of jerky rope hunched in front of my bended knees. At the same instant, Ambrose appeared under my extended hand.

He might have come out of sheer nothingness, as though

160

produced by a super-magician. I was feeling around in empty space, seeking the source of the sounds, when I touched an invisible boot and Kelly's needler spouted across my neck and something promptly went haywire at the back of me and there was Ambrose, flat on his back, bound and gagged. In my state of mind I was so unwilling to accept the evidence of my eyes that I tore off the gag, aimed my needler at him and spoke to the point.

"Maybe you are Ambrose and maybe you aren't. So don't echo my words. Pick a few of your own and say them quick."

I'll say he was a selective picker! What he gave forth made my ears jerk and struck Kelly dumb with admiration. It was fast and fluent and uttered with considerable passion. Usually he was a quiet sort of individual and no one would suspect that he had it in him thus to enrich the language of invective. One thing became certain beyond all doubt: no creature born of this crazy world could have put up such a performance.

Well, I carried on with the job of hacking his bonds which were made of a very tough kind of woven grass, while he continued to voice vitriolic afterthoughts and bring up words he'd previously overlooked. Bits of greasy cable wormed around aimlessly, going nowhere. There were now five faces gaping in the doorway, the others having joined Kelly.

Slinging away his severed bonds, Ambrose stood up, felt himself all over, said to the five, "Have you found Mac?"

"Not yet," replied Wilson.

"Ten to one he's in the next igloo," said Ambrose.

"You lose that bet," Wilson informed. "We've just cased it and he ain't."

"*How* did you go through it?" I chipped in. "Did you nose all over the floor?"

Looking at me as if I were daffy, Wilson asked, "Why the heck should we do that?"

"It'd be a good idea," interjected Kelly, hefting his needler and wetting his lips.

"Look," I said. "You see what you're told to see. And if you're told to see nothing whatsoever——"

"Listen to me," said Ambrose. "These lump of snakes

could kid you into anything." He stepped forward. "Let's have another look through that hut."

Back we traipsed to number fourteen. Six beams lit it up from wall to wall, from floor to roof. Vacant. Empty. Darn it, you could *see* that nobody was there!

Standing in the centre of the single room, Ambrose called, "Mac, can you make a noise, any sort of a noise?"

No answer.

It looked loony, him standing there appealing to somebody less visible than a ghost. I tried to imagine McFarlane lying nearby, straining mightily against his bonds in an effort to create a hearable response, while he remained completely hidden by our own short-circuited optic nerves, kind of buried deep in the blind spot in our brains.

Just then a notion hit me in a way I conceived to be a real spark of genius. The hand-beams pointing in six directions—they illuminated the place much too well!

"Hey!" I said. "Let's aim these lights all the same way."

"What for?" asked Molders.

"Because," I informed, enjoying beating them with applied science, "we're drowning out shadows and if anyone is here they ought to throw shadows."

"Yes, that's right," agreed Wilson, openly admiring my I.Q. "So they should."

Ambrose waved an impatient hand and put me down for the count by saying, "A waste of time. You're as blind to shadows as you are to what causes them. When you're taken for suckers you're taken good and proper."

"Ugh!" grunted Brennand, little liking this assurance. He fondled his pate on which a small bump had risen.

Again addressing the room, Ambrose declaimed, "All right, Mac, if you can't let out a squeak maybe you can roll. I'll stay here. See if you can roll up against my legs." He waited a while, looking down at his boots. Time seemed to suspend itself. Then he gave up, glanced around, caught my inquiring gaze. "I'm going to feel the floor alongside the wall at this end. You do the same at the other end. The rest of you keep tramping around the mid-space. If you kick or knock anything, grab it!"

Dropping onto hands and knees, he commenced crawl-

162

ing beside the wall with one hand seeking forward. I did the same at my end. Having already found Ambrose in somewhat similar a manner it wasn't so eerie an experience for me as it would have been for the others. Nevertheless it still gave me a slight touch of the heebies. There's something upsetting in not being genuinely blind yet knowing that one's eyes can't be depended upon. I'm talking about the effect, of course, not the cause. Nothing was wrong with our eyes either structurally or functionally; the trouble lay farther back where false vision was being imposed and accepted by the brain.

While the others stooged around in the middle I came to a corner, turned and fumbled along the adjoining wall, reached the next corner, made stroking motions through thin air and—*whahoo!*—I touched something invisible, grabbed it, got a handful of cold and slimy rubber pipe. I couldn't let go. The shock of it kind of paralysed me so that I couldn't let go. It made a powerful squirm to get away, hauled me violently forward and I fell on my face.

Kelly used his brains. He'd a slight advantage over the rest, having witnessed the performance next door. Seeing me plunge onto my pan, he directed his needler a foot ahead of my extended fist and let it blast. In half a second there was uproar. I found myself clinging with one hand to a madly sinuous tangle of black rope which strove to lug me toward the door while Kelly cut pieces off it and Brennand rayed its middle.

Ambrose was yelling for someone to give him a knife to cut McFarlane loose. Kli Yang tried to snatch up the alien in a powerful tentacle but couldn't risk losing a lump of himself to a needler. Wilson did a war-dance in the middle of the floor, his weapon fully activated as he aimed it sloppily and let go one flare that somehow passed an eighth of an inch under Kelly's fat rear and another eighth over my hair and burned in the wall a hole the size of a dinner plate. I don't know how he achieved this feat: his ray must have bent a couple of times contrary to every known law.

I let go what I was holding and it left a greyish, smelly slime on my hand. The thing was in little bits by now, with the needlers slicing it smaller and smaller. No matter how much the sections were cut up they still humped around, their raw ends moist and black with little white strings in them. I estimate that in its original knotted-ball form the thing had been about four feet in diameter and weighed one hundred fifty pounds or more.

In the opposite corner McFarlane busied himself casting off lengths of grass cord with which he'd been bound. His expression was sour.

Finishing freeing himself, he griped at Ambrose, "Why didn't you stay in the boat and yell for help?"

"Because your twin brother appeared and beckoned me out as if it were urgent and wouldn't keep," Ambrose informed him. "And because I didn't know then what I know now. So full of misplaced faith I jumped out of the lock and got myself all tied up." He sniffed, added, "I've learned my lesson. Next time I'll sit tight while you die in agony."

"Thanks," said McFarlane. "Someday I'll do as much for you." He spat on what looked like a piece of snake trying to loop itself into a circle near his boot. "Well, do we stand here gabbing all night?"

"It's you who's chewing the fat," said Brennand. He went to the door, pointed his hand-beam the way we'd come. "We'll take you two in the lifeboat. Lift it and get back to the *Marathon* without delay. You can do all your squabbling when——"

His voice cut off, his hand-beam quivered, then he snatched at a side pocket and rapped, "A hundred of 'em! *Flat!*" He threw something while I buried my face in the floor for the second time.

The night lit up briefly but with intense brilliance. The ground gave a twitch and the roof of the hut took off skyward like one of those ancient airplanes. A second or two later wriggly bits rained down from the stars, bounced on the floor, commenced their eternal squirming.

Even if they could make metal things and instruments, the creatures of this world didn't seem to have developed the manufacture of what we regard as weapons. Possibly they'd overlooked this line of progress while spending a million years perfecting their power of deception. Anyway, our powers must have been as alien and unfamiliar to them as theirs were to us—and this latest demonstration

164

of still greater power probably knocked the stuffing out of them.

We rushed out to take full advantage of confusion caused by the bomb, dashed past huts either roofless or slapped cockeyed, and held ourselves ready to sling another bomb should anything real or illusionary appear *en masse*. But no enemy host saw fit to bar out way, no herd of imaginary dinosaurs was planted in our path.

I wondered about the latter as I hustled through the dark with the rest. If I had the ability to make people see things I'd get a guy on the run from a thought-up rogue elephant. But then I realised that the true strength of this power lay in confusing us with familiar things—and these aliens couldn't dig up many items we'd regard as familiar. Any stock illusions they used to maintain mastery over this planet's lesser life-forms would be completely alien to our minds and liable to have a bomb tossed at it. Yes, in dealing with us they were severely limited by lack of knowledge and experience of our particular kind. But if someday they gained a complete understanding of humanity from feet to hair . . . !

Undoubtedly this was their motive in snitching Ambrose and McFarlane. Rule one: get to know the creatures you wish to control. The four men already grabbed were intended to provide necessary data on the strength of which they hoped to take the lot of us. Maybe they could do it too, given the chance. I doubted it, being what I am, but didn't feel inclined to underestimate the opposition.

By this time we were well beyond the encampment and ought to be fairly close to the lifeboat. What with the darkness and the circular arrangement of the huts it hadn't been easy to tell one direction from another. So far as I'm concerned, I'd been content merely to follow the others like a sheep, but Brennand had struck along this line without hesitation and seemed to know where he was going. I started pondering the notion that Brennand might have been impetuous and misled the entire gang. Our pace slowed, became hesitant, as if the same thought had occurred to the others. Surely the lifeboat hadn't been planted as far out as this?

Then Brennand's beam swung round in a searching arc and revealed the lifeboat's tail-end shining metallically on our left. Evidently we must have slanted a few degrees off-track. We went toward it.

Standing by its ladder, Ambrose blinked into our lights, said, "Thanks, fellows. We'll go straight back and see you at the other end."

With that he grabbed the ladder in both hands, made a couple of curious leg motions like a guy riding a non-existent bicycle and dived onto his beak. This looked purposeless and rather silly to me. It's the sort of irrational action that doesn't get you anywhere. Then I became aware that the lifeboat had blanked out as though it had never been and that Ambrose had taken a run at a ladder that wasn't there.

Kli Yang said a word in high-Martian for which there is no Terrestrial equivalent, directed his beam circularly in an effort to find the creature or creatures responsible for this booby-trap. That one or more were within mental range was self-evident—but what was their mental range? Ten yards or a thousand? Anyway, he found nothing but bushes and small trees or objects convincingly like bushes and trees. There was no way of telling short of spending valuable hours burning every individual growth.

Lugging Ambrose to his feet, McFarlane remarked with a touch of malice, "Do you have to fall for them *every* time?"

Thoroughly riled, Ambrose snapped back, "Shut up before I bust you one!"

"You and which other three?" inquired McFarlane, quickly preparing himself for some horsing around.

Shoving between them, Brennand growled, "You two more than anyone else should have the sense to know that by beating each other up you may be playing somebody else's game."

"That's true enough," supported Molders, seeing the point. "Hereafter if any of us gets a sudden desire to knock somebody's block off, he postpones it until we get back to the ship."

"Maybe you've got something," admitted McFarlane, slightly sheepish. He made a gesture. "Anyway, we've something more to worry about. Where's the boat?"

166

"Can't be far away," I opined. "A hundred of them couldn't pick up that tonnage and carry it out of sight."

"We'll circle from this point," Brennand decided. "We're bound to hit it even if we go most of the way round." He gazed in one direction and then the other, temporarily uncertain which best to take.

"Try leftward," suggested Kelly, and thoughtfully added his reason. "I'm turned that way already."

We went left, maintaining our bearing from a faint view of the outer ring of huts barely visible when all our hand-beams were turned toward them. It didn't occur to me that at this stage the huts might be as illusionary as the lifeboat had proved, with the real huts standing unnoticed someplace else. I reckon we could have been persuaded to roam round in rings for the next hundred years. Or even to go in a straight line, thinking we were circling, until we were miles deep into the bush.

Perhaps that bomb had bumped off the sharpest witted of the enemy, leaving the duller ones to miss up chances, for the huts were genuine enough and we found the lifeboat after going four hundred yards. This time Ambrose felt the ladder, went carefully all the way up, fingered the rim of the airlock door, patted the vessel's hull.

"Well, as I was saying before, thanks fellows!"

He unlocked the door and went in, McFarlane following. Shows you how dopey even the cleverest can be at times, because the entire six of us stood there giving them the sweet goodbye with nothing on our minds but that we'd beat it to the pinnace immediately they closed that door. McFarlane did close it, but immediately opened it again, looked down upon us with the superior air of one who occasionally employs his think-box.

Giving us the same sort of pitying smile one bestows on a Venusian guppy, he said, "I suppose none of you want a hitch?"

Brennand gave a little jump and mentioned what should have been too obvious to overlook, "Jeepers, we don't *have* to use the pinnace to go back!"

With that, he bolted up the ladder. The rest followed, me next to last with only Wilson behind. I had to wait a bit to let Kli Yang haul himself inside and get clear of the smallish lock which he'd fill to capacity without help from anyone else. Then I mounted, entered the lock, heard Wilson take the ladder over-eagerly and slip down a couple of steps. Being metal, the treads were liable to toss you onto your head if you treated them with hurried contempt. Out in the dark I saw his hand-beam wave wildly around and extinguish. He had a second go at the ladder while I stood by the closing mechanism.

"You can climb like a giraffe," I jibed as he reached the top and got into the lock.

He didn't choose to crack back, which was unusual to say the least. As I made ready to operate the ladder-fold and shift the door-closing lever, he strolled past me with a fixed expression and exuded a strong smell of grey slime.

There are moments when one must cast aside finer feelings and compunctions. So I kicked him smack in what ought to have been his belly.

And in a flash I had a tangled ball on my hands, rolling and tugging six ways at once, trying to trap my hands in contracting loops, coiling loose ends around my ankles to trip me up and lay me flat. The wild energy in it might have run a dynamo for a week. What with its greasiness and the violence of its movements, I couldn't hold it. Neither could I drag out my needler: it kept me too busy. I'd just gained the grim realisation that I was going to get the worst of this struggle when Kli Yang shoved a tentacle into the lock, snatched up my opponent, smacked him twenty times on the metal floor and slung him out through the still open door.

Without pausing to voice gratitude, I picked up my hand-beam, got a good grip on my needler and went down the ladder in double-quick time. Three or four yards away Wilson was rolling around with two dollops of active rope. Evidently his captors were striving to aim their attention two ways at once, like Martian eyes, but weren't quite able to make it. They were trying to nail Wilson down and fool any would-be rescuers at the same time. Wilson spoiled it by using more than his fair share of their mental concentration and the result was peculiar.

The vision of the struggle kept snapping on and off as if projected by an intermittent movie-dingus. For a couple of seconds I could see them. Then I couldn't. Then they

168

were back again in plain view. I snapped a neat blast at one black thing during a momentary appeareance and severed the loop it had wound round Wilson's face. Then Kli Yang fell off the ladder, belted me aside and joined the hooley.

He was especially well fitted to deal with the situation. Ignoring the visual play of here we are and here we aren't, he curved great tentacles around the area of combat and scooped up the lot, gripping them with powerful suckers. Next he sorted them out, accidentally handing Wilson a thick ear in the process. With one tentacle he dumped Wilson halfway up the ladder while he employed a couple of others to hammer the rope balls upon the ground. He kept this up for quite a while, once or twice changing rhythm to show he wasn't in a rut. Finally he held them in mid-air and walloped them together. By this time the visual switching had ceased. Kli's victims had become decidedly democratic, having no desire to pretend that they were anything else but what they were. He pitched them over a dozen trees.

That done, he followed me up the ladder, squeezed himself into the lock immediately I'd vacated it, closed the door, and sealed the boat. I went forward to tell Ambrose we were all aboard, shipshape and watertight, and that he could blast off.

McFarlane was squatting beside Ambrose in the tiny control-cabin and talking by radio to the pinnace.

"What d'you mean, you'll shoot us down if we take off first?"

The voice from the pinnace said, "If you're returning to the *Marathon* we must be there ahead of you."

"Why?"

"Because we have the list of passwords and they've got to be recited. How do we know who you are?"

Scowling at the instrument board, McFarlane answered, "Yes, yes, that's fair enough—but look at it the reverse way."

"What d'you mean?"

"You bums haven't got any passwords. How will those on the *Marathon* know who you *are?*"

"We haven't left the boat," declared the voice with some show of indignation.

169

"Hah!" sneered McFarlane, perversely enjoying the argument. "We've only *your* word for that."

There was a splutter at the other end, followed by, "Those six agreed to return here. They haven't done so. You say they're on your boat—and we've only *your* word for that!"

Glancing over his shoulder, McFarlane growled at me, "Speak to these crummy boneheads, Sergeant. Tell them you're here complete with a seat in your pants."

It was overheard at the pinnace, for the voice put in sharply, "That you, Sergeant? What's your own password?"

"Nanifani," I elocuted with relish.

"Who else is there?"

"All of us."

"No casualties?"

"No."

A pause for cogitation, then, "All right, we're going back. You follow us. Land after us."

Not liking authoritative instructions from a lower rank, McFarlane bristled. "Listen, I don't take orders from you!"

"Yes you do," contradicted the other, not fazed in the least. "Because this boat is armed and that one isn't. Try anything funny and we blast you wide open. The skipper will kiss us for it!"

Defeated by the truth of that last remark, McFarlane cut off the radio with a savage flip of his thumb and sat glowering into the night. Half a minute later the darkness ahead was split by a crimson streak as the pinnace boosted upward. We watched the flame-trail diminish at about ten thousand feet, then I grabbed the nearest grips and hung on as Ambrose fired the tubes and took her away.

Contrary to our expectations our return didn't cause any panic while they tried to decide whether we really were what we looked to be. I wouldn't have been surprised if they'd subjected me to a series of tests designed to prove absolute and indisputable Terrestrialism. Fingerprints, blood-checks, and so forth. But they had reduced it to a technique far simpler and easier than that. All we had to do was walk aboard and pause in the lock while Jay Score gave us the once-over.

170

Inside the *Marathon* it was obvious that the ship was held ready for departure. We weren't staying long. Going to the washroom, I had a hard job getting grey slime off my hands: it smeared and smelled and tended to kill the foam on the soap. Next I made a quick check of the armoury, found everything in order. If we took off before long things would be busy for a while, so now was the time to get the latest information from Steve or anybody willing to gossip. Couple of yards along the passage I met Jepson and gave him the sinister haha.

"So you're still in a state of animation. What happened?"

"I got picked on," he said without pleasure.

"Natch. You ought to be used to it by now."

He sniffed and commented, "I'd have some hopes of getting used to it if it occurred the same way each time. It's the variety of methods that gets me down."

"How'd it come this time?"

"I was mooching through the woods with Painter. We were separated from the others but not far from the ship. Painter saw or thought he saw what looked like a kind of metal ornament on the ground and he dropped a few steps behind as he stopped to pick it up. According to him, his fingers closed around nothing."

"And then?"

"Somebody cracked his head while he was bending. I heard him flop, turned around. I swear I saw him still standing there and holding whatever he'd found. So back I went for a look and—*bam!*"

"Same treatment as he got."

"Yes. Painter says a tree did it, but I don't know. I came around, found myself bound hand and foot, with a wad of grass strapped over my kisser. I was being dragged head-first though the bush by a couple of slimy nightmares." He made a face. "They had to be seen to be believed."

"I've seen 'em," I assured. "But it wasn't until they took off their pyjamas."

"They dumped me, went away, brought back Painter similarly fastened. Then they beat it toward the boat, presumably for more clients. We lay there helpless until lights flashed, needlers flared, there was a bit of a hullabaloo and the search party found us. The boys said they'd destroyed half a dozen things that looked like trees to them but not to Jay Score. Jay strode around and picked them out for gunning."

"Old Camera-eyes, eh?"

"That's the way he is—and it's lucky for us we've got him aboard. Prize mugs we could be if we had to go around with no choice but to accept whatever we saw."

"A means will be found to combat it," I assured. "They milk me of taxes to support bulgy-brains in laboratories and I'm not chancing my neck around the cosmos for nothing. So if they want my hard-earned dough they'll have to build me a wire-hat or some other contraption that'll stop me going dreamy in a place like this."

"The next crew to land here will need wire hats all right!" he endorsed, then continued on his way.

I found Steve gnawing a dog biscuit in his cupboard and asked, "What's doing? If you know. And you know everything, Bigears."

"Don't you know?" he retorted. "Of course you don't. You know nothing, Peabrain."

"Okay." I leaned on his doorjamb. "Now that the formal introductions are over, what's the dope?"

"We're zooming when everybody's safe aboard and Mc-Nulty has viewed their reports."

"So soon? We haven't been here more than a day."

"Want to stick around?" He cocked an inquiring eye.

"Heck, no!"

"Me, neither. Quicker I get back, the quicker a nice, thick wad will be pushed at me."

"We haven't found out so darned much though," I objected.

"The skipper thinks we've got as much as is wanted," he gave back. Putting his feet up on the rim of his radio desk, he settled himself comfortably and went on, "Certain smarties on Earth pick a planet by the simple expedient of shutting their eyes and throwing a dart at a star-map. They say that's where high-life may lurk and we'd better go take a look. All we need to discover is whether the dart scored a hit and what the high-life is like. Those two items we now know—so home we go before heads are torn off and insides pulled out."

"Suits me with one reservation," I told him. "And that is expressible in two words, namely, never again!"

"Hey-hey! You said that last time."

"Maybe I did, but——"

The ship howled, I cut off the conversation, took it on the run to my harness and just managed to survive the departure. I'd never become used to the way the *Marathon* came and went even if I experienced it a thousand times. A secret desire of mine was to subject Flettner to a few stiff doses of his own inventive ability.

We were some twenty million miles out when Bannister stuck his head into the armoury and inquired, "What was eating Mac when he yapped from the lifeboat? He sounded like I'd no right to speak to him."

"This is a guess, but I think he was being egged on to cause trouble. The old divide and rule gag on an alien plane. But it didn't work because he was too civilised to carry it that far."

"H'm! I hadn't thought of that." He scratched his head, looked impressed. "Ingenious, weren't they?"

"Too much for my liking."

"I support that sentiment. I'd hate to dream that any of them were on board. Imagine being bottled with a bunch of guys or not-guys or maybe-guys and you can't tell who from which."

"The idea can be developed further and more intimately," I said, having already given it much thought. "That is if you care to scare yourself."

He gave me a funny sort of grin, half humorous, half apprehensive, and finished, "I can scare easier by watching those educated spiders in the starboard lock."

With that he departed and I continued with various jobs. Now that he'd mentioned them, my mind shifted to the Martians, a tentacular life-form fully as alien as anything we'd met. But we were thoroughly accustomed to them, so much so that we'd miss them if they dropped dead. Yes, the Martians were good guys. Everybody liked them. Nobody was scared of them.

Then why Bannister's strange remark? And why his uneasy, lopsided smirk? Seemed to me he was drawing my attention to some illegal capers now taking place in the Martian refuge from thick air. This thought grew on me, giving me the fidgets, until I had to drop what I was doing and go take a look.

What I saw when I applied my eyes to the small spy-hole made my back hairs jerk erect. The Red Planet gang were clustered as usual around a chess-board, all except Sug Farn who lay snoring in one corner. At one side of the board was Kli Dreen, his saucerish attention on the chess pieces as if his eyes were joined to them by invisible thread. I noticed that he was playing white.

Facing him, a big ball of greasy black rope put out an end of itself, touched a black bishop but didn't move it. The Martians took in a deep breath as though something had actually happened.

Yowee! I didn't wait to see more. I went toward the bow so fast my heel-plates struck sparks as I skidded round corners. The last bend I took the same time as Jay Score coming the opposite way, with the result that I cannoned into him full tilt. It felt like diving into a cliff. He grasped me with one powerful hand, burned brilliant eyes upon me.

"Something wrong, Sergeant?"

"You bet!" I absorbed the five-fingered feel of his grip to reassure myself that he matched his looks and I wasn't being kidded. I said, slightly breathless, "They're on board."

"Who are?"

"Those oily, coily hypnotists. Or one of them, anyway. It's fooling the Martians."

"How?"

"It's duping them at the chess-board."

"I doubt it," he said, evenly and undisturbed. "It hasn't had sufficient time to learn the game."

"You mean——?" I gaped at him. "You *know* it's here?

"Of course. I captured it myself. Then Kli Morg begged it off me, pointing out that it couldn't escape from their double-locked low-pressure joint. That's quite correct, though it wasn't his real reason."

"No?" I felt considerably deflated. "What was his reason?"

"You should guess it, knowing that crowd. They think they may get a run for their money at chess from a thing that can visibly move one piece but actually move an-

174

other." He mused a moment. "That means they'll have to regard every apparent move with suspicion and try to identify the real one as a logical probability. It should bring a new element into the game and lend it a certain extra fascination."

"Do you really think so?"

"Most certainly."

I gave up. If the Red Planet gang had a crazy obsession, he shared it enough to understand it and actually connive in it. Someday he'd win himself a Martian championship vase of violent colour and revolting shape that I wouldn't stand beside my rocking chair as a gobboon.

Space-conquerors, bah! Nutty, all of them, just like you and me!

THE END